HEATHER BOYD

BESTSELLING AUTHOR

MISS MAYHEM ✦ BOOK 4

MISS MERTON'S LAST HOPE

The characters and events portrayed in this book are fictitious. Any similarity to real persons, living or dead, is purely coincidental and not intended by the author.

Chapter One

High overhead, seagulls squawked but the chill in the air marked the approach of the cold season. The ocean was quiet today, but it wouldn't be that way for long. Winter was coming and the old fishermen predicted a harsh season ahead. Walter George relished the idea of many a night home alone reading a good book, preferably his sister's next, and writing to friends after they left for their distant homes while the wind rattled his windows. "It's going to be quiet around here soon."

"Not so quiet with us remaining." Valentine Merton grinned. "Julia and I talked it over last night and have decided we *will* stay for Christmas. My parents need more time to accept our marriage."

During the last summer, Valentine had accepted the challenge of racing Julia to prove that a woman could swim as fast as a man, and lost. While he had not suffered for being beaten by a mere slip of a girl, Julia had certainly not been celebrated for her success. She had been ostracized and criticized by all and sundry. Their marriage last month had lessened the scandal somewhat, but still, not everyone was prepared to let the matter rest, especially Valentine's parents.

Mrs. Julia Merton was lovely but her habit of unconventional behavior still turned heads, even among friends. "I had hoped your sister could convince them to accept the marriage and that would be the end of it."

To everyone's surprise, particularly Walter's, Melanie Merton, Valentine's younger sister, had been a staunch supporter of the match.

"There is still some ways to go." Valentine grinned. "I have to hand it to Melanie, she knew just what to write to bring them around to at least be civil. '*She just needs the correct example to follow*'. Despite the promises in her weekly letters, there hasn't been one lesson to improve Julia since father left Brighton."

Walter smothered a laugh at Valentine's imitation of his sister's voice. The man was a *long* way off. "It must be crowded for a pair of newlyweds to have a sister underfoot."

"They seem to rub together well enough. I never imagined Melanie would hand the running of the house over to my wife so easily, but I suppose it helps that we are hardly ever at home during the day. The shop is another reason for missing out on the family festivities, if you could call them that."

Walter would not like to spend a Christmas with the elder Mertons himself. From all he'd discerned of their gatherings, they were as merry as having a tooth pulled. "I have rarely seen you pair except in the evenings or early morning. It pleases me that you're both so dedicated."

"I must earn a living, and I want to." Valentine glanced at him slyly as they strolled along. "And unfortunately, I have the most overbearing landlord to satisfy. Such a taskmaster he is. Never gives a fellow a moment of peace."

Since he was the landlord, the new owner of Valentine's building, Walter let the complaint roll off his shoulders. "I've come by less often than once a week, thank you very much."

"I know." Valentine smiled slowly and glanced about them. "Do you know the last month has been the most satisfying of my life?"

"You do seem uncommonly content." Walter glanced away. The man was positively smug of late. Not that he blamed him one bit. He was newly married.

He sighed a little wistfully then shook off the sensation that he was the odd man out. He was healthy. He was wealthy. He had no need for anything except perhaps a little companionship now and then.

Valentine rubbed his hands together briskly. "All I need next is to see my sister happily married."

Walter nodded, as he was expected to do when the subject of marrying sisters off came up in conversation. His own sister had married a neighbor and friend so he had plenty of experience in this field.

He considered the lady under discussion. She was lovely in her own way, tall, perfect complexion, a beauty, but she wasn't the least bit approachable. "A tricky proposition, in your case. How many proposals has she turned down?"

"Oh, eleven, I think it is."

Walter grunted, surprised by the number. He'd only heard of a handful of local beaus who had been turned down. "That many?"

"Be a friend and don't spread that about. I'm still hoping for one more who might be acceptable before we get to unlucky number thirteen."

Walter shook his head, unable to fathom why Miss Melanie Merton was so damn particular about choosing a husband. He was acquainted with a few of her former suitors and they were all quite decent sorts and intelligent enough to please even her father. None had possessed a great fortune or a title. "Maybe number twelve will suit."

"One can only hope. Otherwise she might find herself with a husband not of her own choosing. Now I'm married, our parents might turn their attention on her, and I shudder to think whom they'd pick for her amongst the Oxford crowd. She should find someone she at least likes." Valentine frowned. "Not that I want to send her packing again, but I don't like that she is alone so much."

Valentine had sent Melanie away before his marriage. The few months she'd been gone had changed her, in Walter's opinion.

"You know, I'm damned if I can work out why she refused the last one. The one before I sent her away," Valentine clarified. "Alexander Anderson was a decent sort, nice tidy fortune; she seemed easy with his family too. We were all expecting something more, but when the time came, she turned him down like all the others."

Walter had expected that match too. "Has she fallen in love with someone you wouldn't approve of?"

Valentine started to chuckle. "I've never had one moment of worry about her behavior, so no, I have no fears that she's set her cap for an unsuitable fellow."

Across the beach, two of the Clemens boys were playing catch. A fast toss sailed past the smallest one, rolled toward Walter, and fell inside a footprint in the sand. Since the boy didn't immediately see where it stopped, Walter ran forward a few steps and picked it up. "Missing this, Jimmy?"

"Oh, thank you, Mr. George," Jimmy said before closing the gap between them. "I would have been skinned alive if I'd lost it."

He ruffled the boy's hair. "I doubt it will come to that. Better run along now and finish your game."

Valentine shook his head. "I can never remember all the Clemenses' names."

"Well, I pay attention, and I have spent far more time here than you have." He knew everyone in Brighton, and when a new family arrived he made it a point to introduce himself as soon as possible. "So you've *never* caught your sister and a suitor misbehaving?"

"I'm starting to wonder if she considers men in that fashion."

"Then she's nothing like *my* sister." Walter smiled, thinking of Imogen and her unabashed interest in the male species, one in particular—her husband, Sir Peter Watson. "I overlooked a great deal because I was certain she and Sir Peter were headed for the altar. And if they'd not ended up there of their own accord, well, there is a nice reef offshore where I could have dumped our baronet for a very long swim as he rethought the consequences of his actions."

Valentine laughed as he pulled on his boots then slung his damp towel over his shoulder. "At least with Imogen, you knew if the right man came round she'd make her feelings clear to you. And I highly doubt your threat against Sir Peter. You're doing it much too brown, my friend."

He wasn't quite as affable as everyone liked to make out, but he didn't care to argue the point. He had been very serious about that reef. If Peter had hurt Imogen's feelings, toyed with her affections a second time, he'd been ready to put the man in this place. "Imogen has never held back on expressing an opinion, but about Sir Peter she was particularly stubborn."

"Much like Melanie." Valentine stopped. "Do you remember how close they used to be?"

Melanie and Imogen had once been the best of friends. Inseparable as children. "Long time ago that was. They hardly speak now."

"I wish…" Valentine stared out to sea. "I sometimes wish Melanie and Imogen were still on good terms. She was happy then. Do you recall what they fought about?"

Walter glanced at Valentine sharply. "There was no disagreement. Melanie simply stopped speaking to Imogen. One summer they were as close as two peas in a pod and the next time she came to Brighton, Melanie acted as if she was too important for my sister." *And for everyone else.* "Imogen cried for weeks because of those snubs."

"I'm sorry," Valentine murmured. "I don't remember why she would have done it either."

Since fathoming Melanie Merton's mind wasn't in his best interests, he turned for home.

Walter had lived in Brighton his whole life and he thought no other place suited his temperament more. He had traveled to London and beyond a few times, but here, he had his favorite shops, good friends and family close by, and the sea to watch and swim in on a daily basis if the weather allowed.

Along the shoreline, young families dotted the space and were setting up chairs and blankets to enjoy the sun while it lasted, laughing and playing as if nothing could ever hurt them. He *did* remember a time when his sister and Melanie Merton had been exactly that way. He could still recall their heads pressed together, their arms casually draped around each other's shoulders as they played their silly games and shared secrets. His mother and Melanie's old governess had occasionally had to lock doors to keep the pair apart on the longest days of the year.

But that was years ago, before Melanie's old governess had died. She had not ever been so full of high spirits since then. "What was her old governess's name?"

"Mrs. Anderson."

"No, that's not quite how I remember it," he said slowly.

"Melanie called her Andy didn't she?"

"Yes, I believe you're correct."

Walter stopped and glanced out to sea, seeing those days with a touch of nostalgia. Melanie had adored Andy and she'd changed so much *after* the woman had passed away.

He shook his head as nostalgia shifted into a new perception of past events. He'd never quite put the two events together until now. Was Melanie's withdrawal because of the governess's death? The woman employed to replace Mrs. Anderson had been very strict about everything. Was that all it had taken to end a friendship?

"We're having an intimate dinner with friends tomorrow night," Valentine said as their street came into view. "You're invited, of course."

Walter smiled ruefully. "I don't mind being the man to make up the numbers provided there's a good dessert to be had at the end."

"Why do you think I invite you along to dine with us so often?" Valentine slapped his shoulder. "You seem to be the only man within three miles who hasn't the least bit of interest in Melanie romantically. I am always assured Melanie has an enjoyable evening in your company."

Walter was surprised by that claim. He had always assumed his presence made little impression on her mood. He could have stood on his head, for all the notice she took of him. "Who else is on the guest list?"

"Mr. Hartwood and his wife have consented to come."

"I know them well, but they are an unusual choice as Julia's first dinner guests."

"The choice was my sister's suggestion, actually," Valentine confessed. "She thought a series of small, informal dinners would strike the right note to win back goodwill. Plus it's an opportunity to casually promote the shop to someone with funds to spare."

"Clever thinking." Despite the frost in her manner, her choosiness about finding a husband, Melanie was well regarded by the older set of their town. She had certainly been of help in improving Valentine and Julia's standing in society of late. "As good a place to expend the effort as any I can think of."

"She is determined that Julia make a good impression."

His mind jerked back to Melanie Merton and her refused suitors. Why did she not want a husband of her own yet? As far as he could tell, she rebuffed all romantic overtures. Had any of those fellows ever stood a chance to win her affections? Had any of them kissed her?

She could probably use a good kiss to loosen her corset strings. Walter imagined…

"Why are you pursing your lips?" Valentine asked suddenly.

"What?" He quickly adopted a thoughtful expression. "Oh, just thinking an idea through. There's a factory in Portslade I heard about. Could be a good investment."

Valentine stopped and stared at him. "How do you have money to spare for another investment already? I swear, everything you touch must turn to gold."

"Not quite." He grinned. "I am still eating off porcelain dinnerware."

Valentine questioned him about the property while Walter scolded himself silently. It was a very bad idea to turn his mind to Melanie Merton, a woman who had hurt his sister so very badly in the past. Despite the friendly façade he affected before others, he was still extremely annoyed with her. Luckily, he wasn't the sort of man she would ever notice was constantly biting his tongue rather than sharing his real feelings.

Chapter Two

Melanie Merton hated her life. She hated the clothes she wore. The house she lived in that was no longer hers to manage. The smiles she had to bestow upon her brother's friends while overlooking their scowls. Even without the responsibilities she'd always enjoyed, and the hours on her own, she never had a moment's peace. She just wanted a quiet morning, and that never seemed to happen lately unless she confined herself to her bedchamber.

Today, she was entertaining Mr. Linus Radley until his sister, Julia, her new sister-in-law, came down that morning. The forms of proper behavior that had been drilled into her head since she was a young girl made it impossible for her to say what was really on her mind, even when she wanted to. She was too polite to ask Mr. Radley to go away until a more reasonable hour of the day, and had ordered tea and cake to fill the endless minutes until Julia relieved her of this duty.

"It looks to be a lovely day for a stroll," Mr. Radley said suddenly. "Might I entice you to venture out with me to look upon the sea? With your maid, of course."

Melanie sighed with what she hoped sounded like regret and not irritation. She would not go out walking with Linus Radley, with or without a suitable chaperone. She had seen enough of him in the past weeks not to want anything more to do with him than she absolutely had to. He was a bully. "Unfortunately, I am otherwise engaged today."

"Oh?"

Dear God, the man wants particulars. She searched her mind for the least interesting activity she could think of that might dissuade his interest. Mention of a charitable project always seemed to bore most gentlemen into leaving her presence. "I am to visit the vicar in an hour to discuss the needs of the poor. I do what I can in my own small way but there are so many families in need. I truly hope some kind and generous benefactor comes forward soon."

As hoped, the mention of money and needy families blunted Linus Radley's interest in the subject. He asked no more questions and indeed seemed decidedly uncomfortable in his chair. She'd never met a more tight-fisted man and his inclination to help those less fortunate wasn't anything ever boasted about. She glanced at the clock. Almost ten. Julia was truly dragging her feet.

Melanie poured a second cup of tea for Mr. Radley but then discovered there was not enough for a second cup for herself.

"Will my sister be joining us soon, do you think?"

She smiled. Thinking fondly of her sister-in-law was easier now that they'd spent a little more time together. Julia had her moments but rising early without prompting from Valentine wasn't one of them, apparently. Linus, being Julia's brother, should have known of her inclination for late starts. Yet here he was, sitting expectantly in her company. "Our maid assured me she would be along soon."

"And your brother is out?"

"Yes, swimming, as is his usual habit." She handed him a cup. "I thought you would have joined him and the others."

"Not today." He set his cup aside untouched. "I cannot lie any longer. It was really *you* I wanted to speak with. I have a favor, a question to ask you if I might, and it is quite a personal matter, so please forgive my unconventional calling hour."

"Oh," Melanie said, but inside she groaned. She did not want to do him any favors. She simply wanted him to go away. Instead, she said, "How can I help?"

"I'd like you to be my wife."

His statement, and his eager smile, caught her off-guard. A marriage proposal from Mr. Radley was the last situation she ever imagined herself in when she rose this morning. She forced her breath to calm, to not snap "absolutely not". She held her tongue those precious few moments and all for the sake of peace within her family. She didn't really like him but she hadn't wanted to reveal the depths of her loathing.

"You are overcome," he murmured, and then he switched seats to sit at her side. "I completely understand, but you should not be surprised."

She was not overcome; she was in shock. This would be her twelfth refusal—and possibly the most awkward. Linus Radley was family by virtue of their siblings' marriage. Melanie had turned down enough suitors that the necessary words sprang from her lips easily. She did not want children of her own although everyone expected her to marry and do her duty. Her only recourse was outright denial of any man's suit so she would avoid conception altogether. "Mr. Radley, while I appreciate the honor you do me, I cannot accept."

His mouth fell open. "Excuse me?"

The idea of a woman refusing to marry wasn't as easily accepted as she might wish. If she ever dared hint at a disinterest in bearing offspring, she was usually stared at as if she were out of her mind. She had learned, early in her life, to keep her feelings about the matter to herself as a consequence. Usually she claimed other reasons for her refusal, and would again today.

"You have long been my brother's friend and you are family since his marriage to your sister. We have been acquainted many years and while I have always thought very well of you, I do not believe we would suit as husband and wife."

His jaw set and Melanie could see hints of his temper rising. This she also knew about him, from Julia and Valentine's passing comments about Julia's life before her marriage.

A volatile man would not suit her as a husband if she were ever inclined to marry. She did not approve of men who could fly into a rage so easily as to make a woman afraid. She did not fear

Linus, but she would never place her well-being in the keeping of a temperamental man.

She folded her hands in her lap and patiently waited for him to understand her refusal was final, and there was nothing left to do but to take his leave.

"I see." He glanced around, his eyes narrowing. "So you are nothing but a heartless tease."

Melanie gaped at him. "I am not. Why would you say such a thing?"

"We are alone, and have been alone on many occasions in the past weeks since your return. Do you not think you make a man hope for a more intimate acquaintance, given your behavior?"

"You are family." She stood, infuriated that her kindness had been twisted into something she'd never once intended or imagined. "I had no thoughts of a change in our relationship beyond ensuring your comfort in my brother's home."

Linus stood too, moving closer so they were eye to eye. His nostrils flared as he raked her with a harsh glance. "I think you like the attention of so many men dangling after you."

She blanched at his accusation and took a pace back. She did her best to dissuade the most insistent of gentlemen callers by any means necessary. She had been very inventive. "I do not."

"Then why flirt with every man you meet to the point where so many have proposed, only to decline them?" Radley took another pace toward her and her breath came too fast at the look in his eye. "Do you imagine yourself irresistible to all, but so far above us that our feelings matter so little? You must know everyone expects us to wed."

She shook her head violently. "That is untrue. No one expects it."

"Everyone expects a match to be made between us. Who else would you marry?"

Of all the nerve. She was almost rendered speechless by the suggestion. Almost. "I will not marry to please other people."

"The size of your dowry and your beauty can only grant you so much latitude. Remember that when you throw your wiles at the next handsome man who comes calling on you."

Melanie was astounded by his arrogance. He was passably

handsome but no more than many men. "You flatter yourself."

Her words had no affect.

"You might not find life with an ill-favored man as comfortable as with me. But then, it is always the overparticular ones who die alone and miserable."

"Radley! Apologize!"

Melanie jumped at the force behind the outraged demand. At the door, Valentine and Mr. George stood slightly unkempt after their trip to the sea. To her surprise, it had been Mr. George who'd spoken and demanded the apology. She'd never heard him speak quite so loudly before, and the expression of fury on his face was quite unfamiliar too.

Valentine appeared stunned, but she hurried to him because he was her brother and she felt safer far away from Linus Radley.

"What has happened?" Valentine asked her quietly, catching her fingers in his. Melanie cringed and wiggled free of the grip. She certainly had never enjoyed confessing she'd turned down a suitor before, and this time was far worse than any other. She knew her brother hoped she'd find her own life, her own happiness one day, but it certainly wouldn't be with Linus Radley, given all he'd just said to her.

She took a breath to start the confession, but Mr. George cut her off with a softly spoken murmur, "I think number twelve is just as unlucky as the eleven prior suitors for your sister's hand."

Melanie shrank behind Valentine as she realized her romantic life, or lack thereof, was a subject of discussion among their neighbors. Men did talk and, over the years, Melanie had certainly given them ample proof she was particular in that regard. It was just rather horrible to hear Walter George could know the exact number of men she'd refused. She had not imagined Valentine would have told anyone.

Valentine took a pace toward Linus. "If my sister has refused you then I imagine your business here today is done. If you'd be so kind as to apologize for your outburst and be on your way, there is no need to ever discuss this matter again."

Linus tossed his head arrogantly. "I will not apologize. It would have been a good match, if her vanity weren't so overblown. You said it yourself more than once, she will end up an old maid before she finds a husband she deems worthy of her hand."

Valentine's jaw clenched. "Sir, you go too far to think you have the right to speak for me."

"Oh, come now," Linus shot back. "I only voice what you have alluded to over the years."

Valentine stayed silent and Melanie wrapped her arms around her chest, hurt to the quick. Valentine must think the same if he didn't deny Mr. Radley's words. Had she made a mistake in staying in Brighton?

"I think I see the problem," Walter George said as he glanced between them all, his eyes narrowing. "You're family, and you certainly don't care to upset the applecart when it has only just started to roll along smoothly again."

"Oh, shut up," Mr. Radley snapped at him.

Rather than be intimidated, Mr. George stepped forward. "You should apologize to Miss Merton now."

Melanie shivered at the menace in his tone. She'd never heard that from him before either.

"What has this to do with you, George?"

Mr. George set his hands to his hips. "If you consider yourself in any way a gentleman, you will retract your words before this goes any further. Remember, I'm *not* family and I have the luxury of not caring that I offend you, especially when you are so far in the wrong."

"This is none of your concern."

"If I have to teach you a lesson in manners, so be it." He dropped his hands to his sides but the next moment they curled into fists.

"She led me on," Mr. Radley insisted.

"That is utterly ridiculous." With one punch, Mr. George knocked Mr. Radley backward.

Melanie cried out in shock, but Radley quickly righted himself and lifted his fists.

"No!" She caught Walter by the back of his coat to drag him back across the room, noticing as she did that Valentine had tackled Mr. Radley and was forcing him in the direction of the door. "What are you doing?"

Thankfully, the large man yielded and backed up a few steps. "Defending your honor seemed appropriate. I always thought Radley had a vulgar manner about him when it came to the ladies. I don't blame any woman for turning down such a man." His gaze sharpened on Mr. Radley. "Do not speak to her again until you can do so as a gentleman."

"Walter!" She could not believe such words would come out of the quiet man's mouth. He was normally the least excitable out of all of her brother's friends.

Valentine finished shoving Radley out the door and slammed it shut. He turned to them and his face was pale. "Hell."

"Valentine?" Julia asked in a worried voice from the staircase. "What's all the noise?"

Melanie cringed as Valentine approached his new wife. He caught her hands in his. "Your brother proposed to Melanie and was refused. He took it badly."

Julia's face brightened into a happy smile and she hurried across the room toward her. "Oh, well of course you would refuse him, Melanie dear. You haven't the slightest symmetry of thought in your entire being, and he would make you utterly miserable as a husband. I would have protested the match myself, and vigorously too. He is not good enough for you."

The moment Julia embraced her, Melanie cringed inside and yearned for release. However, Julia persisted and they hugged awkwardly a few moments longer.

"You shouldn't have hit him," Valentine maintained, staring at Walter George. "I would have preferred not to subject my sister to such violence."

"Well, clearly you were trying to keep the peace and he had it coming." Mr. George met her gaze and he frowned. "He wasn't going to apologize. He always did tend to petulance when he didn't get his own way."

Julia giggled behind her hand. "I could not have said it better. It was never me who threw a tantrum."

"No, you dove out the window instead and ran to Imogen for sympathy and advice whenever you were in trouble," Melanie said without any malice. Julia had always run away from her problems but Melanie didn't have that luxury. She would face them alone.

Melanie turned away. This mess was all her fault. If she had stuck to propriety she would not have created such a scene. She had forgotten that, while new to being family, Linus Radley was also a bachelor and she an unattached woman.

She flinched as Valentine put his arm around her shoulders and gently escorted her to the front hall. They had gone months without touching, but she could always expect such an action when she'd turned down another suitor. He undoubtedly thought the gesture of affection would make her feel better. She was relieved when he released her and stepped away to collect his hat and gloves from the entrance table.

"I'll go and talk to him and perhaps this mess will blow over sooner rather than later. He is family and you will have to see him at some point. I wouldn't like any lingering unpleasantness to mar the upcoming holiday season."

"I understand." The thought of seeing Linus Radley again over the Christmas dinner table turned her stomach into knots, but she'd face him when the time came and hide her dislike yet again.

"Come along, Julia," Valentine grumbled. "Let's see what fences are left to mend this time."

The door closed rather ominously behind them and Melanie was grateful. Her legs began to tremble, but she refused to allow a complete collapse. A refused proposal was one thing, familiar though unpleasant, but a private brawl afterward was beyond the pale. She might never live down this shame.

Chapter Three

<hr>

Walter waited until the front door closed behind Valentine and Julia then caught Melanie's elbow to steer her back into the parlor before she fell over in a faint. She was pale and trembling beneath his hand and he was actually worried about her state of mind. "Are you all right?"

She jumped as if she'd forgotten his presence until he'd spoken and shrugged off his grip to stand alone. "Of course. As unpleasant as that was, I am glad it is over and in the past."

Walter didn't place much faith in her words. He was acquainted with her well enough to spot a false smile a mile away. He stepped toward her and she edged back quickly, confirming for him that she found proximity to others extremely unwelcome. Had anyone ever delved deep enough to find out why she continually rebuffed family and friends? "You know my character, Melanie. You have nothing to fear from me."

Her gaze darted to his guiltily and then she nodded.

He reached for her trembling fingers and caught them in his. "Just imagine we are about to dance. You've held on to me many a night for that."

"I have." She turned into him, her other hand rising to his shoulder as if they were about to step off into a waltz together. They were actually very good at that, having partnered each other for so many years.

She took a few quick breaths and settled herself again.

When he judged her calmer, he smiled. "I have a question."

Her hand jerked back from his shoulder. "Oh, please, not you too."

He stared as her face pinked, unsure at first how to respond. Surely she did not think that he was about to propose? He wasn't an idiot. In her current state, she wasn't thinking clearly. Walter shook of his irritation. "Never fear, I only want to ask a question that's been on my mind of late and will not rest."

She stared at him and then she swallowed. "Anything."

"Where were you when your governess died?"

She glanced away to hide her face. "I was at home of course. In Oxford."

"I knew that." Walter firmed his grip on her hand and slid the other into position around her back. It was surprisingly easy to hold her like this, pretending to dance when what he really intended was to question her. "But where in your parents' house?"

Utter terror flickered over what little of her face he could see, but then she swiftly masked it behind a polite smile he'd seen so often. The change in Melanie stopped his heart. Was he close to uncovering the mystery of her alteration? He took a step and she moved with him, lulled by the familiar situation.

She might not like him to presume, but he knew without any doubt he had to wait on her answer, or he wouldn't ever understand the woman. And to his surprise, he very much wanted to. He took another step, then another, diverting her around a chair so they would not stumble.

She had slid her hand into position on his shoulder again but those fingers trembled still, revealing her anxiety over the question as clearly as if she'd spoken an answer. She might not like him to assume he had the right, but he thought at that moment Melanie Merton desperately needed to unburden herself.

She stared at the pin in his cravat while her fingers wriggled in his grip as if she were fighting her own instincts to flee. Indeed, her next words were the softest of whispers. "Why do you ask me that now, of all times?"

"I have perhaps just destroyed a friendship to defend your honor, and I want to know it wasn't without a very good reason. I do not deny you the right to refuse a proposal of marriage, but there have been eleven other spurred suitors over the years. Most were decent men of good social standing who your father would have approved of."

She nodded and her hand smoothed over his shoulder.

He drew her closer, widening his fingers on her back. "Today, I could not help but notice you shy away from any comfort offered, even by Valentine. You were not always this way. You were my sister's best friend once, and now you barely speak. As a girl you were held often, and comforted others when they were in need. Julia once came to *you* when she'd hurt herself on one of her misadventures, rather than to Imogen. So did Imogen."

She stiffened as soon as he reminded her of those happier times, so he took another step to distract her. "Tell me what happened. It was after your Andy's death, after you returned to Brighton with a new governess we all hated, that I think you started to change toward us."

She inhaled raggedly and she stumbled forward, something she'd never done while dancing with him in public. She hadn't stumbled even during practice as a little girl. "I didn't know."

Walter pulled her into his chest, dropping the pretense of dancing. "Tell me, Mellie?"

She sniffed at the use of her childish nickname. He hadn't used it in a long time, but that name had once echoed through all the houses of her friends in Cavendish Place. Not since the days before Andy had died, in fact, had a little girl called Mellie run about and laughed with them. After that unexpected death, this reserved creature had begun to walk among them and had turned aside every overture of familiarity.

Until he'd taken the initiative today.

"I was supposed to keep out of the servants' quarters, but I hadn't seen her for days. I snuck upstairs and into her room after my parents had gone out for the night to an entertainment at the university. I was young and wanting a cuddle so I climbed upon her bed and she let me come into her arms. Her breath was very loud and strained. She hugged me tight against her and I didn't want her to let me go. She told me she loved me and after a while she fell silent." She dropped her head to his chest. "I was only supposed to stay a moment and then I was to go back to the nursery where I belonged."

Walter wrapped both arms about her and held her against him, suspecting what she would say next if she could bring herself to that point. He'd seen a corpse or two, his parents' faces in death were still with him, but he'd been older when they had died and had been able to distract himself with the arrangements for their burials and in comforting Imogen. But a child of Melanie's age then might not have been able to push it from her mind so easily.

At last she said, "I fell asleep there in her arms and she died holding me."

Walter closed his eyes briefly, heart breaking for her. Valentine had never spoken of the servant's death. Did he even realize what had happened to Melanie that night? "That must have been a shock when you woke."

She shuddered and jerked back out of reach. Her lashes were wet with tears and she looked about to fall to pieces. It took a long time before she spoke again and her words were raw, hard with pain. "I couldn't get free of her grip, she held me so tightly."

And so now she lets no one close at all. She can't bear to let anyone comfort her.

He brushed a tear from her cheek carefully. Her soft skin was hot and he struggled against the urge to pull her back into his arms. He'd found the reason for her withdrawal and at last he understood what had begun the change. "I am so sorry."

"I thought at first she was playing a game and begged her to let me go before anyone found me and, and...when fought free, I turned. I did not recognize her." Melanie sobbed the last words and she began to shake again. "Her eyes were open and...I was so terrified that I fled to the nursery without telling anyone she had passed away. I didn't want to get in trouble. I didn't know everyone expected her to die."

"You did nothing wrong," he assured her.

Fresh sobs shook her and he inched closer. "She loved you very much. I remember that. I can understand that you didn't want her to be alone when she was ill."

"I wasn't allowed to love her, but I did." She sniffed. "She was the only one who dared to risk my parents' ire. If a servant was too familiar with us, they were dismissed without a reference. They couldn't be bothered with me except when they had guests to present me to."

"'They' being your parents?" Walter was fast learning to detest them. He stroked the backs of his fingers down her hot cheek once more. "There is no harm in loving the people who look after us. Those brave souls who live with us every day, expecting no more gratitude than the coin they are paid. For good or ill, they shape our lives in ways our parents could not ever imagine sometimes."

He moved his hand to rest lightly on her shoulder. "You were only a child and what you saw of Andy's death must have been horrifying to you. Her last moments on earth were spent with you. She would have died happy."

"Perhaps." She wiped at her eyes. "But I cannot forget."

"Then don't try to."

Her face lifted to his and the expression there broke his heart. "If only I had been good and done as my parents had told me, if I had remembered my station, then I would never have to remember her like that. I did not mourn her," she whispered. "I huddled in my room and hated her for not sending me away."

Walter took a risk and bent his head to rest against hers. What she had witnessed, what she had suffered in silence, guilt and horror and mourning all confused about in a child's mind, had changed this woman from the happy girl she'd been once. She had loved deeply and mourned still. It was no wonder even friends were rebuffed. Melanie simply couldn't bear to let anyone that close again.

He sighed at the pain she'd hidden behind excessive propriety. "Then honor her memory but don't let her passing torment you. She was a wonderful woman and you were always a good girl, always her favorite."

He did not say she was good now because, to be brutally truthful, Melanie often spoke harshly of other women when they failed to meet her high standards. Was that too a result of her grief? Her terror of letting anyone close again? Hiding how lonely she must be behind a strict adherence to rules and propriety?

Her head twisted a little against his, brushing her soft hair against his skin. "I am not that girl anymore. I don't feel as other women do and I'm not sure I even know how to be any different than I am."

"At least you know you have faults," Walter murmured. "Most people live oblivious to their mistakes."

"And I have made so many." Melanie sobbed again but beneath the whimpers, the sound of the front door shutting reached him. He drew back, assuming her brother had returned.

"There is no reason you cannot overcome this," he promised her. "When you turned away from Imogen, she thought it was her doing. She loved you so very much once. You could have her friendship back if you just try. We all liked Andy a great deal. If you explain, talk about how tortured your feelings were by her passing, Imogen would understand. Andy was a kind woman and she spoiled you as if you were her own daughter."

"She was the only one who ever loved me."

"Everyone loved you," he insisted. "You should tell your brother what happened with Andy. He needs to understand why you spurn your suitors and don't like to be touched. He could help you overcome your fear."

"Perhaps one day, but I don't think now is the time. He's likely to be more concerned with smoothing over this latest curfuffle with Mr. Radley than digging up the past when it no longer matters to anyone but me."

"Oh, Melanie. Radley can go to hell before I'd ever place his happiness above yours."

Valentine's voice jerked Melanie away from Walter and her gaze darted to the door where Valentine stood, tears slipping down his cheeks. "There's nothing more important than you."

Walter glanced away to pretend he'd not seen his friend's raw emotions.

"I did not know you had come back."

Melanie's usually firm voice trembled and Walter wanted nothing more than to reach for her hand again but couldn't. However, he was glad Valentine had eavesdropped. It was important that he know what drove his sister to the extreme desire to be proper every moment of her day. She was not the heartless tease Linus claimed. She was not cold, nor unfeeling. She was in many ways still that little girl and clearly still grieving for the mother she never really had.

"That was intentional, and I am glad I waited to hear it all before interrupting what on first glance seemed an entirely different situation." Valentine sent a pointed glance his way and stepped toward his sister. He tilted her face to his, his touch gentle and slow, and wiped away another of her tears. "You should have told me long ago about Andy. We could have talked about it and maybe things could have been easier for you."

Melanie said nothing to that and he appreciated that Val didn't push her to agree with him. It was time for Melanie to stop pretending everything was all right.

He glanced at the doorway to find Julia standing there frozen, just out of Melanie's line of sight. Her face was contorted with upset. She slipped her hand over her mouth and edged away silently. Walter applauded her decision because he didn't believe Melanie would appreciate the fuss. Not everyone was lucky enough to have the warm and loving childhood they'd experienced.

He glanced back at Valentine in time to see him raise his arms to embrace Melanie then think better of it. He patted her shoulder instead. "I was coming to tell you that Julia and I could not find her brother and we've decided not to bother. He was rude to you in a way that is unforgivable. I held back out of concern for Julia's feelings for him, but as it happens, she rather wished *she'd* had a chance to thump him as our Walter here did on your behalf."

Walter laughed and earned a disapproving frown from Melanie. It had been a rash act on his part but entirely satisfying. He flexed his fingers, noticing a slight ache in them.

"I don't need to be cossetted, Valentine, nor to have my spurned suitors beaten up by interfering neighbors." Melanie straightened her spine, once again trying to appear unaffected. Walter saw through the act. "This thing with Mr. Radley will blow over in time and as to Andy, it was a long time ago."

"But not for me. We have a great deal to talk about. You were not the only one who loved Andy. I missed her too. She was the only one we had when we were young. We should have talked about her instead of pretending we didn't miss her."

Melanie nodded slowly, though she didn't seem altogether pleased. "If you wish."

Walter took that as his cue to make himself scarce. "I'll be on my way."

Valentine faced him. "I would appreciate your discretion."

"You don't even have to ask." He nodded to Melanie. "Good day, Miss Merton."

"Good day, Mr. George."

Valentine showed him to the door with a steady pressure to his back. It was hard to ignore the feeling he was being forcibly removed from the house. He supposed he deserved it, since he had been sticking his nose into Merton family secrets. He collected his hat, gloves and damp towel.

"Do you wish to speak to me about your interest in my sister?" Valentine asked once they were out of earshot and the front door stood open.

Walter turned. "I don't have any interest in her."

"Then remember the sisters rule still applies to mine and keep a distance," Valentine warned. "I don't wish her reputation ruined and the pair of you miserable."

The door shut in his face slowly and Walter stood there a moment in shock.

Good God, had the world gone mad? He wasn't interested in Melanie Merton in that way. She'd tolerated his questions today because her guard had been lowered by other events, but things would return to normal. Tomorrow she would ignore his existence. There was nothing of which he was more certain.

Chapter Four

---◆---

Melanie slept beyond her usual rising hour the next day. She felt drained of all feeling but strangely better about her life. She hadn't dreamed; not one nightmare about Andy to wake her in a cold sweat while others slept peacefully.

She had told her brother everything that she remembered about the day their governess had died. The coldness of Andy's skin, the scent and stillness of her quarters, her anguish over the loss of the servant who had mothered her every day of her life.

Her heart had grown lighter as they'd spoken and when she glanced across her room to the marks on the old wood-framed door, notations of how tall she'd grown each summer, the longing for Andy had faded to regret.

Like so many small comforts, the marking of her height each summer had stopped with Andy's death.

Mother and Father had immediately replaced Andy with a stern spinster who'd never shown her any affection. Melanie had been forced to smile even with her broken heart, and soon enough she'd learned not to react to the pain of Andy's loss.

But she had never forgotten the love she'd had wrenched away so suddenly.

After Andy's death, her parents had insisted her toys be packed away and, at Mother's insistence, Melanie had concentrated on learning how to run a home from then till now. She'd been thirteen when she'd played hostess at her first dinner party for the chancellor of Oxford in the place of her absent mother. She'd been so anxious about the seating arrangements she'd made herself ill.

Valentine had wept over what she'd endured in Andy's room and made her promise not to tease him about it later.

She would never tease him. Not when he held her future in his hands. He alone had the final say on when and if she had to return to their parents' cold home. When she was there, her nightmares, memories of Andy's passing, were strongest and worst.

She uncurled herself from her bed and began to dress, knowing the maid would most likely be with Julia at this hour. When she was presentable, she stepped out into the hall in search of her breakfast.

She paused at the top of the stairs when she heard Julia groan. Since Julia had married her brother, Melanie had discovered sounds of that nature could occur for any number of reasons. She just hoped Julia wasn't stuck half in, half out of a window again.

After determining the sound had indeed come from her brother's bedchamber, a room the newlywed pair now shared, she reconsidered investigating. At this time of day, her brother should already be out at his shop, but it never hurt to be cautious. The pair often enjoyed a leisurely affectionate farewell most mornings, or a test of strength that involved a great deal of huffing and puffing. She'd peeked into their bedchamber once to her own peril, to find Julia pinning her brother down, and then she'd kissed him so passionately that Melanie had been embarrassed and fled silently all the way outside the house. After that, she'd done her best to give them every chance for privacy.

However, given the doorway was open wide, Melanie considered it safe enough to take a chance. She tapped on the wall as she moved along the hall, just loud enough to give warning of her approach.

"Come in, Melanie dearest, and good morning," Julia sang out.

She took a few steps in and glanced around, relieved not to find her brother lurking about the bed. That bed was covered in Julia's gowns and several had been tossed aside very carelessly. Julia herself was sitting at her dressing table twisting her head this way and that to see herself in the mirror, but her hair…

Melanie moved toward her new sister. "What have you done to yourself?"

"I wanted to try something new." Julia had at last tamed every strand of her bright-red hair, forcing it back into the tightest of styles that could be managed. "Do you like it?"

The style was very similar to the way Melanie wore her own straight hair but it didn't suit Julia one bit. It was too severe and, with her fair complexion, she appeared so much older than her actual years. It was simply awful. She could not be seen like this.

Julia had always been sensitive about her appearance though, even more so since the scandal, so she chose her words carefully. "What made you change styles?"

Julia glanced up quickly and caught her hand in a quick squeeze. "I was thinking of the bargain we made with your parents. They expect me to be as ladylike as you, an asset to the family, and I thought I should make an effort."

The gown she wore was very plain and if memory served, was a gown rarely worn. It was a dowdy gown and all wrong for the vivacious Julia. Melanie had to stop this before the girl had no pride in herself left.

Melanie smiled softly. "Ladylike behavior is what they expect, but how you style your hair and clothes are a completely personal matter, in my opinion. The way you've always worn your hair and dressed suits you better. Might I change you back?"

Julia's gaze dropped, but she eventually nodded. "That is very kind of you."

No doubt Julia was disappointed that her decisions had been unsupported, but in the long-term it would be for the best.

Melanie made short work of releasing Julia's hair from confinement then spent some time brushing the snarls created by her earlier treatment. Her sister-in-law had hair as independent as its owner, and the curls soon bounced back into place with a bit of effort. Then she twisted and pinned Julia's hair into a loose chignon, noticing the immediate improvement to her beauty.

When she was satisfied with her work, she lightly pressed her hands on Julia's shoulders. "There. Back to your usual pretty self, the way my brother loves you best. Are you headed for the shop today?"

"No." A tinge of color swept over Julia's cheeks at the mention of Valentine and his obvious affection, so Melanie rang the bell and then made a fuss of straightening her dresser into order again until the moment passed. "Mr. Faraday is expected to visit so Valentine suggested I could stay at home and allow them to talk freely."

"Stand up and let me help you out of that rag then." She ran her gaze over the bed and picked out a pretty gown accented in pink ribbon and delicate lace. She would look very fine in that for morning calls.

Their maid appeared and Melanie stepped aside so Julia could be changed. When Julia was free of the plain gown, Melanie requested it and rolled it into a ball. "Never wear this again. I cannot bear it."

"Yes, Melanie."

The maid suppressed a relieved smile and took the gown away when Melanie handed it over. When they were alone again, she caught Julia's chin gently. "Beautiful. You have such a lovely figure and you should always wear the clothes that accentuate your beauty rather than hide it."

Julia's fingers crept into hers and squeezed. "I am very glad to have you as a sister, Melanie."

"I am glad too. No one could love my brother more." Melanie moved back a bit and found the pocket watch that Valentine had given Julia on their engagement. She pinned it to her waist and slipped it into the hidden pocket they'd fashioned for the purpose of holding it securely. "I was on my way downstairs."

Enthusiastic as always, Julia snatched up a light shawl. "What were you going to do today?"

She had little to do, in truth. Julia's presence denied her many responsibilities and she was finding it hard to fill the hours of her days. "After breakfast, I was going to read today's paper if Valentine did not take it with him. And, if there are no callers, I will resume my embroidery."

Melanie hoped no one came today.

Julia slumped against the bedpost. "Embroidery again? Please, please don't suggest I join you in that."

Melanie chuckled softly. Sitting still for the morning was not Julia's favorite activity. And when she did turn her attention to her embroidery, Julia often ended up stabbing her needle into her finger more times than into the piece she'd been assaulting. The complaints were endless. "I would never suggest it. Perhaps we could convince Valentine to take you for a stroll along the shore when he comes back."

"We have not decided on Lady Watson's birthday gift as yet. Last year she was a miss and now she's a baroness. I have no idea what to give her this year. Her party is the day after tomorrow."

"Yes, I remember." That was a party she wasn't invited to, not that she didn't understand why Imogen would exclude her. She didn't deserve an invitation, not after the way she'd behaved. Walter might have suggested making up for past mistakes would be easy, but in her experience, it was terribly hard. She didn't know how to even start with Imogen.

Julia twirled a red curl around her finger. "What about dance instruction as something to do today? You wrote your parents that you could help me prepare for the Oxford Ball next year and Imogen is sure to want to dance at her party. I should practice."

Melanie winced. Dancing would deny her the quiet morning she'd been hoping for, but this was not her house anymore. Julia was mistress of it now and her own needs came second. "I told my parents a great many things. There really isn't anything wrong with your method."

"But I'm not as graceful as you." Julia nodded. "You look very elegant when you dance. I don't want to embarrass the family when we do visit Oxford."

Melanie thought a moment. "All you really need to do is be a little less enthusiastic. You're supposed to let your partner lead you, not you lead him around the dance floor."

Julia winced. "I'll have to practice. Valentine will be home soon. I want him to see that I'm trying."

Melanie stared at Julia, a girl she'd once dismissed as hopelessly wild but now saw simply had lacked a good example to mimic and someone to please. She was willing to try to change a little and all because of Valentine's love.

The discovery made her feel a trifle envious. There was no one she'd change herself for; well, not so far. There wasn't one man who had sincerely tried to claim even the tiniest portion of her heart, and as had been pointed out yesterday, there might never be. That fact should comfort her, but it didn't. After all, she was trying to avoid becoming a wife. "Very well, we can practice dancing today."

Julia clapped her hands. "This is going to be so much fun. Thank you."

Chapter Five

---◆---

"You are not getting out of here without taking a turn," Valentine whispered as the sound of the pianoforte once again filled the room with beautiful sound. The parlor had been cleared for dancing and Valentine's wife was waiting in the center for a partner to come back to her, looking incredibly lovely and altogether anxious. Why Valentine wanted another man here was a complete mystery. He should want to be alone with his wife.

Well, more or less alone.

Walter cast a second glance at the other occupant in the room. Always lovely, always elegant and unruffled, Melanie Merton had largely ignored his arrival in favor of choosing music to play. "What do you need *me* for?"

Valentine frowned. "To keep Melanie company while we dance."

He raised a brow. His head was still spinning from Valentine's accusations yesterday that he was interested in Melanie. He most assuredly was not. Yesterday he'd done no more for her than he would have done for any of his friends' sisters. And then today, he'd only stopped in on his way back from the vicar's because he'd heard the music.

However, discovering an impromptu dance lesson in progress had been too amusing to walk away from immediately, so he had stayed a while. A decision now he should perhaps regret. "Will I be accused of having designs on her later?"

"Of course not. I don't know what I was thinking to say that. You're a good friend to all of us. I'm very lucky she's so comfortable around you that you managed to find out what troubled her."

"Fortunate timing. Nothing more. I caught her at a weak moment." Walter shrugged.

"Please. A reprieve for my toes is needed," Valentine whispered. "I don't know why Melanie allowed this."

"The Oxford Ball is important to your parents. Besides, how could Melanie say no to what your wife wants? It is Julia's home now and this is how it's supposed to be," Walter murmured out the side of his mouth.

Valentine appeared startled by his observation and stared across the room. "Do you think she's upset about that too?"

"How could I know, but it doesn't take a brilliant mind to see the situation has changed due to your marriage. The ladies are smiling at each other still so I don't believe there's anything to worry about. Let me tell you now, though, that it is not easy to be the odd man or woman around newlyweds."

He moved toward Julia. What could it hurt to stay a while longer? "Mrs. Merton, forgive my presumption but would you be agreeable to having tea sent in? Dancing is thirsty work and I understand you've had a very busy day so far."

Julia Merton grabbed her husband by the hand and towed him back to the center of the room. "If you insist."

"That is a fine idea, Mr. George," Melanie said, glancing up swiftly at the squabbling couple then back down to the keys with a frown. "Or any moment there might be no marriage," she muttered.

He laughed quietly so the warring spouses didn't hear and hurried to find the housekeeper, who was more than happy to serve something very quickly to ensure the peace was kept.

When he returned, he caught Melanie staring at her brother and his wife as they bickered over whose fault the latest stubbed toe was with such a strange expression on her face that he froze. She appeared almost wistful. He hoped bringing up the past as he had yesterday hadn't been a mistake.

Her head snapped around and she spotted him staring at her. She chose new music and set it precisely before her.

He stopped close to her and she began to play, one eye on the keys, one on her brother and sister-in-law as they fumbled through the steps of a waltz. Over the years, Imogen had dragged him to many a public recital, but the ones he had enjoyed most always included Melanie's performances. She played so effortlessly he couldn't help being impressed, even when he'd wanted to find fault with her for that too.

Valentine winced and started to hop. The music ceased.

"Forgotten how to dance, Val?" he teased.

The look Valentine sent him was pure irritation. "I would dance perfectly well if my wife would let me."

That remark brought a chill into the new bride's expression. He moved nearer to them, puzzled at how two people so obviously in love could not perform the simple function of dancing together. Julia was one of his favorite partners. She wasn't at all relaxing, but she certainly did know the steps of every dance.

He bowed to her extravagantly and held out his hand. "May I?"

Val backed away quickly with a disgusted scowl and Melanie commenced to play once more. As he'd expected, Julia followed his lead but he did need to keep a firm grip and force her to bend to his pace and style of dancing. After a few turns about the room, he bent his head. "You're doing well," he whispered.

"Tell *him* that," she grumbled.

Her posture changed after her words and he quickly guessed she was much too tense to enjoy herself. When he'd danced with her before the marriage, she'd been bubbling over with excitement at every step, but now she was trying much too hard. "My dear, could you ease your grip on my hand the tiniest amount? You have nothing to prove to me."

She bit her lip and glanced past his shoulder to where her husband stood waiting with such a tortured expression that he brought them to a halt again. She winced and whispered, "Do you think he regrets he could not have done better?"

Walter had thought the marriage had ended Julia's doubts, but apparently not. "Stuff and nonsense. Since you are asking me, I think you are exactly what he needed in a wife. He'd be much too boring otherwise."

"I'll never be as elegant as Melanie." Her shoulders sagged. "I'm a disaster."

"If you were beyond help, he would probably love you more." He glanced up and met Melanie's gaze over Julia's shoulder. "He would be a fool to want you to mimic her. You have as many worthy accomplishments as she does."

Julia blushed. "I wish I'd had you for a brother instead of Linus. Imogen was so lucky to have you in her life."

"She would laugh to hear you say such an outrageous thing and come after me with pins to deflate my ego." He smiled as he caught Melanie watching them, her frown proving she was trying very hard to hear their conversation. "My sister only sees my faults."

"What are they again?" Julia asked and then laughed, and the moment of dissatisfaction on her part appeared to pass.

After a time, Melanie surrendered her position at the instrument to Valentine and as he took up the tune, she stepped up behind Julia. "Relax your shoulders, Julia dear."

Julia took a breath and her shoulders dipped the smallest amount. Walter's ability to lead seemed now less of a struggle with Melanie guiding his partner.

He nodded slowly, pleased with the change. "You see, only a little adjustment is needed. Dancing, like marriage I suppose, is an act of faith and compromise. Just be yourself and all will be well."

Melanie's eyes widened momentarily at his bold words. He'd seen enough of marriages, good and bad, to make that suggestion. When two parties in a marriage refused to yield their opinion and make allowances for an opposing point of view, the union always suffered for it.

He spun them to a gentle stop. "Valentine, your turn."

Julia's shoulders sprang back up.

Melanie moved back into position behind Julia, set her hands on her shoulders until Valentine had taken his place. Walter did not play an instrument so he clapped out a beat he hoped they could move easily to. With Melanie's help, the newly wed couple's next steps seemed a great deal smoother. Melanie joined him near the windows soon after and watched the pair in comfortable silence.

He leaned close. "What do you think?"

"They need to practice more often together, but I think they've made progress. Thank you for reassuring her."

"My pleasure." He paused a moment as the Merton's spun by. "Shall we join them?"

"Here? There'll be no accompaniment."

He ceased clapping but the newlyweds continued despite the silence, at last in harmony on the dance floor. He hoped it held.

"Why not? If we join them, surely they will keep dancing too. Besides, we've danced together since you were six. I imagine we could do it with our eyes closed."

He brought Melanie into his arms, perfectly ready to dance in their usual fashion. Melanie was a very good dancer, she let him lead, and he found her rather a soothing partner.

Her eyes fluttered shut as they moved and he was astonished. "What are you doing?"

"Testing your theory."

A few turns later, he was surprised to feel himself grow self-conscious. He was used to her trust on the dance floor, but not her complete surrender to his control. As they moved around the room silently, an urge to tug her closer into his arms grew. Her eyelashes were very long and dark across her cheeks. He widened his fingers on her back and with a subtle pressure, drew her closer than he would normally do in public. A small huff was all the rebuke he received and he made no further changes.

She glanced up at him at last and licked her lips.

A shock of pure desire filled him and he tightened his grip on her hand as every futile, improper thought he'd ever harbored swamped him at once. He should not, could not, think that way about her. Not ever. He tore his gaze away to stare over her head until the feelings passed.

When the rattle of the tea tray forced them apart, Melanie rushed away to serve everyone and he was very glad for the distance. She didn't look him over with a frown when she delivered his cup, but he thought her strangely agitated.

He couldn't understand what had changed to make him feel desire for her, of all women. It made him feel uneasy and strange and self-conscious. He wasn't the sort of man she would look at twice, and neither should he consider her in that manner. There was much about her he didn't like, particularly her prickly, cutting demeanor.

When she sat, she chose a chair far away from him but kept peeking at him. Had she guessed the direction his thoughts had taken?

He worked hard to suppress his confusion as he sipped his tea, made exactly as he liked it without the bother of being asked to decide what went in. He stared at the cup a moment, realizing Melanie drank hers exactly the same.

That discovery left him with an awkward awareness of Melanie that made his whole body tingle.

Chapter Six

Since the dance lessons were clearly over for the day, Melanie's attention drifted to Walter George again as he assisted with righting the room's furniture back to its normal placement. He had stayed, danced with her again after tea, and seemed in no hurry to go about his own business.

Melanie didn't mind that Walter was here, but the quality of her thoughts relating to him confused her. He was a fine dancer, an entertaining conversationalist. His sense of humor had smoothed over the tension building between her brother and his wife. She liked him.

She *liked* Walter George very much, and that was altogether baffling to realize after being acquainted with him for so long and thinking nothing more of it until he'd pulled her closer in their dance.

When their eyes had met and held, she'd almost swooned at the heat in them. Only her training had saved her from reacting; only her understanding of Walter's character had prevented her from jerking back. The moment had quickly passed and since then he'd been nothing but a perfect gentleman. The same Walter she'd always known and trusted.

Although yesterday when he'd held her, her heart *had* beaten a little faster than she was accustomed to in his presence. She hadn't even minded him prying about her governess's death. He had seemed to possess a genuine interest in understanding her reactions, her need to avoid being held. He would tell no one of her emotional outburst too. He'd promised and she believed him completely in that regard.

Walter had always been a man of his word.

He was possessed of an exemplary character. Very loyal to his friends and family.

She fussed with straightening the sheet music, surreptitiously noticing his ease and affability with her family. Walter was everyone's friend. People just seemed to like him, fathers, mothers, sons, though she'd never heard of him having a sweetheart of his own.

Perhaps it was his ready smile, offered so often in the recent weeks that made her notice his qualities now. Despite all she'd done wrong in the past, all the toes she'd trod on unwittingly, he still seemed willing to be friendly toward her. The first to overlook her many mistakes.

She wasn't really sure why he would want to.

"Are they straight yet?"

His question brought a wave of heat to her face and she quickly set the sheets in a neat pile, and closed the lid over the keys. She normally did not stand around contemplating the appeal, or not, of her brother's closest friends. "I'll just put them away."

She nudged the stool beneath the pianoforte and hurried to place the sheet music in Valentine's study where they belonged on the high shelf. Footsteps followed her and a shiver raced over her skin. She set the music away then faced the room. Walter George had followed her.

"Yes?"

His lips twisted into a slow grin. "Thank you for the dance."

"A pleasure." Her heartbeat quickened as she held his gaze.

"Was it?"

"Yes, of course."

"I had wondered, after yesterday, if you'd have rather not danced. I trust I did not make you feel too uncomfortable."

She shook her head to reassure him. While in his arms, she

had thought about his proximity, but it had certainly not distressed her. "You are a fine dancer, sir. I do not think the lesson would have ended so well without your presence."

He smiled again. "You tested my theory that we could dance together even with our eyes closed. What was your opinion?"

"I was curious but it seemed no hardship to me." She blushed, remembering the feeling of spinning out of control in Walter's sure grip. It had been a wonderful sensation. Almost like floating in the sea, which she hadn't done in years. Not since she'd been a girl in Andy's care. "Did you close your eyes, too?"

"No, I was much too busy making sure to avoid crashing into your brother and Julia. Perhaps another time when they are less unpredictable." He glanced behind him and frowned.

Wondering what it was that drew his notice, she moved to his side, just as his attention returned to her.

His eyes lit with teasing light that set her instantly at ease. "Your brother and sister-in-law have just crept upstairs, no doubt for a private word about the dancing."

She frowned at the news. "They do sneak away fairly often. I suppose that is why Mr. Radley formed the idea that I was *interested* in him. I never considered the consequences properly. Please understand it's not by my design that we are left alone."

"Oh, I am well aware of that," he whispered. His fingers rose to caress her cheek. His thumb stroked over her skin and she blushed, suddenly hot and uncomfortable and all too aware of him as a man. "But I cannot say I am disappointed."

She gaped and then snapped her mouth shut. Was Walter flirting with her? Since he'd never done so before, she wasn't sure what to think or do, or how to account for it. But she was actually more often alone with him than she'd ever been with Linus Radley. She eased back against the wall, away from him.

Walter grinned and took a place at her side then set his hands behind his back so he leaned upon them. He stared at the window and a frown creased his brow. "Julia worries a lot more than I'd imagined."

Melanie relaxed. She was merely imagining his interest. Walter would not have the least idea to be improper. He probably meant nothing by those smiles. He was a friend, perhaps more so than prior to her confession about her governess.

However he viewed her, she appreciated his steady presence and wondered if she could ask more of him to risk confiding further. There had been many times she'd longed for someone to talk to. She leaned toward him, hoping she hadn't misunderstood his kindness. "This morning, I happened upon her before she'd left her bedchamber and had to insist she change her appearance. She'd pulled all her hair back and wore the most modest gown she owned. I am sure my brother would not have liked to see her that way."

He glanced toward the door. "She believes she must imitate you?"

"I had hoped I had imagined it, but after this morning, I do not doubt." Melanie pressed her hands together at her waist. "I don't know how to reassure her that the way she has always appeared is best. Perhaps your sister could visit more often and lend her voice as well. Since the marriage, Julia has not been herself. I fear my father's criticisms have been taken too much to heart."

"Keep doing what you're doing, but I will have a quiet word to Imogen about your fears." He smiled. "I am glad she listened to you this morning. She did look lovely, as do you."

"Thank you," she said, but her heart fluttered. She'd been complimented for her looks all her life, but this was the first time in a very long time she felt certain the compliment was offered with no hidden motive. "You're very kind."

"As are you. You stepped aside very graciously when your brother married."

"It was only right. Julia is his wife and this is her home now."

"It cannot be easy." He turned and leaned his shoulder against the wall, facing her. "You must be very frustrated."

She stared at him. "How could you suggest that?"

"I have been acquainted with you for over fifteen years, and you do like to be busy and do things your way." He smiled. "That was a compliment, in case you were not certain of my intent. I have a high regard for women who know their own minds."

His gaze dropped and her breath caught. Why was he looking at her mouth? "Thank you," she managed to choke out.

"Dance with me again," he whispered.

He held out one hand and even as she slipped her palm over his instinctively, she wondered why she would do it. There was no music. Her hand rose to his shoulder as he wrapped one arm around her waist. Her breath caught as he tugged her closer, forcing her to look at him.

He held her gaze a moment longer than comfortable—and when he bent his head and brushed his lips across hers, Melanie was utterly surprised. And not just by the kiss, but by the fact that it was Walter George delivering it.

He'd tricked her!

Unfortunately, she couldn't make herself move away from him.

She stood frozen in place, her feet rooted to the spot, her lips molding to his.

His kiss deepened to one of gentle exploration. Their lips clung and she couldn't stop the sound that escaped her control.

He drew back, searching her face. A question lingering in his gaze that she had no answer to. She didn't know what he was doing; she didn't know what she was thinking to allow it either.

He cupped her face and brushed his thumb over her cheekbone. His touch was soothing, unhurried, reminding her of his gentleness of the day before.

His other hand firmed across the curve of her back and he sighed softly.

She blushed and glanced down at his chest. She'd rarely allowed a suitor such liberties, for good reason, and Walter was not one of those—never a suitor. In fact, she should stop him before he regretted his actions. She lifted her face to ask for release just as he pulled her against his body and sought her lips again for another kiss.

The kiss was deeper, overpowering, and Melanie clung to him for balance, swept away by an experience unlike any other.

She had allowed a kiss or two from one prior suitor but hadn't particularly cared for the experience of being pawed at. But with Walter, she felt no fear, only familiarity. His tongue danced across her parted lips and she whimpered at the unexpected sensation.

She pushed at his chest firmly, at last remembering where they stood. Valentine and Julia could come back at any moment and she dreaded to think what they might say of her behavior. They might insist Walter had to marry her, just because of a mere kiss. She would refuse him, of course. Walter did not realize he was making a grave mistake.

They studied each other a long moment in silence. Words failed Melanie as she struggled to contain her panic.

Walter nodded finally then cleared his throat. "Thank you again for the dance. I don't believe I've ever had a more enjoyable afternoon."

His gaze darted to her lips once more and she trembled anew. What had she done? Anticipation and fear gripped her. She couldn't decide which affected her more. Walter was just Walter. Her neighbor. Her brother's friend. He had never once shown romantic interest in her before today. She had to say something cutting to send him away, but words stuck in her throat.

"Until dinner tonight, Mellie. Perhaps you might oblige me with another dance then." As he departed the room, a tiny smile lifted the corners of his mouth.

Melanie collapsed against the wall, acutely aware that despite the surprisingly pleasant kiss, she'd dread his return later. She didn't want to disappoint him but she would. She had no business encouraging any man.

Chapter Seven

The trouble with eating with friends was that it was entirely possible to eat too much and not feel guilty about it. That lack of guilt was what had led to Walter's larger size years ago. In recent times, exercise had combatted the worst of his past overindulgence, but hadn't lessened his sweet tooth.

Much like his interest in kissing Melanie. Once tried, it was all he could think about.

He scraped the last of the Empress Pudding from his plate and glanced about him with a warm smile. It was good to be among friends.

Across the table, one of the most influential couples in Brighton was seated and appeared happy. Mr. and Mrs. Hartwood, an older couple with children grown enough to have children of their own, were not quite finished with the splendid dessert course the Mertons had provided. Julia and Valentine were clearly done and smiled at each other all too often. Melanie, his dinner companion, was keeping pace with Walter and had helped along the conversation when it had lagged all through the meal.

Of their earlier kiss, she showed no outward sign of reaction to him.

Mrs. Hartwood pressed a napkin to her lips. "You set a

wonderful table, Mrs. Merton."

Julia beamed happily as Valentine caught her hand. "Thank you, Mrs. Hartwood. You are very kind to say so, but you should also thank my dear sister. Without Melanie's help, I would never have managed it all so well. My brother rarely entertained."

"Well, you are in good hands now." Mrs. Hartwood glanced at Melanie approvingly. "You must both come for tea tomorrow and meet my grandchildren."

Melanie smiled warmly at Julia and allowed her to answer. "We should like that very much."

Such a gracious woman to defer to a younger sibling-by-marriage, but he supposed that was how it was meant to be in such a household. He cast a glance over Melanie and saw more that appealed to him. She was wearing a modest burgundy gown with dark seed pearls decorating the neckline and silver embroidery across the bodice and capped sleeves. It was a simple gown really, but made unique by the careful details, and one that suited Melanie to perfection. She did not try to draw attention but she claimed it anyway.

One had to look hard to see the effort the woman made to suit the situation. Julia, seated across the table, outshone Melanie with her gold necklace and elaborate curls. Her gown was of cream silk and lace, a costly gown by any standard. But of the two, Walter preferred Melanie.

After their kiss that afternoon, he was afraid that he preferred Melanie very much indeed.

He'd gone for a very long walk after their kiss to clear his head, to talk some sense into his galloping heart. He'd listed everything that was wrong with Melanie Merton in his head, and yet still he burned for her.

She was haughty, opinionated and standoffish.

He was astonished with himself that none of those failings mattered so much anymore.

He knew she could do better, he knew he wasn't as distinguished as her past suitors.

But, all that aside, the woman had kissed him back!

He knew what was required, of course. A gentleman did not carelessly kiss a woman like Melanie Merton without holding himself accountable. And he wanted to kiss her again. Soon and often.

So he'd written to David Hawke in London and requested advice in setting up his affairs for a marriage he'd never anticipated.

"Word has it you had an eventful week, Miss Merton," Mrs. Hartwood murmured.

Melanie set down her spoon carefully as all eyes turned her way. "To what do you refer, madam?"

But Walter had an idea. He'd been waiting for this moment with dread all night. Linus Radley had not been slow to gossip at the tavern they frequented, and he had not painted Melanie in a favorable light because she'd spurned him. A wrong response could put Melanie on the outs very easily.

"Why, the proposal of marriage from Mr. Linus Radley," Mr. Hartwood cut in. "It is all anyone can talk about."

She winced. "You've heard?"

Mrs. Hartwood appeared honestly worried. "Heard and been dismayed."

Walter relaxed a little at her words. "A regrettable incident," he murmured, thinking of striking Linus Radley. At the time he hadn't known what had come over him to make him react so strongly, but no woman deserved spite just because she did not agree with a man.

Mrs. Hartwood frowned in confusion. "Do you regret turning him down?"

"Not at all." Melanie drew herself up. "I am simply sorry he misunderstood my overtures of friendship to mean more than an honest desire to be polite. Through my brother's marriage, he is family."

"How extraordinary." Mrs. Hartwood glanced at her husband. "When I heard from those who gossip about such things that you, of all young ladies, were supposed to have led him on to the point of proposing, I couldn't credit it for anything but a mistaken report. It's hardly in your nature to be scandalous."

"My sister acted appropriately at all times, I assure you," Valentine insisted. "Radley is quite in the wrong."

"I believe you. A most unpleasant development." Mrs.

Hartwood nodded then turned to Walter, and the matter was dropped. "I hear you bought that lovely little cottage on Russell Road. Are you finally ready to settle down, sir?"

"I *am* settled. Here, or rather, next door."

"A man is not settled until he marries," Mrs. Hartwood glanced around the table with a knowing smile, "and has a babe to hold in each arm."

"In due time." He'd heard every variation on the topic before, of course, but as one of the last bachelor's in his circle of friends, the discussions about marriage were now rather pointedly aimed at him. "I will marry when the time is right, and rest assured I will call on you to help keep an eye on all the little Georges one day."

Mrs. Hartwood clapped her hands in delight and all around the table were smiles and good-natured support for that suggestion. Over the years he'd found half-truths more satisfying a response when it came to marriage, rather than outright denial. "I will not live in the Russell Road home, but lease it out after repairs are completed."

Mr. Hartwood huffed. "Again, sir, you have beaten me to a property I wanted."

Walter grinned. "I assure you it was not done intentionally, but what is clear to me is that we both have excellent taste in property."

Mrs. Hartwood soothed her husband. "Forgive Hartwood. He's still grumbling over losing out to you over the Forsythe house all those years ago."

"What's this about the Forsythe house?" Valentine interrupted. "My mother's family lived there when I was a boy."

"I own it." He eyed the remaining dessert. Empress Pudding was a favorite and one of the Mertons' cook's specialties. He had not managed to convince the cook to share the recipe but he would one day soon. "Is anyone going to eat that?"

Mrs. Hartwood immediately declined, and silenced her husband with a stern look when he appeared to be about to accept. Everyone else remained silent so he glanced around—to see varying degrees of astonishment on Valentine's and Melanie's faces.

Melanie gasped. "Since when?"

"The house? Oh, the property was my very first investment." Although it was no great secret, Walter considered his property investments, and his wealth to be no ones business but his own. Mr. Merton senior had dispensed with the property for a song long ago without one trace of hesitation, and had actually set him on the path of his own small fortune. He glanced at Valentine curiously. "Did your father not tell you of the sale?"

Valentine glanced at Melanie instead of answering him. "No wonder he has refused to discuss the house," Valentine murmured to her.

"Ah. The Forsythe property was in quite a state the first day I walked in as owner. A leak in the roof had ruined the ceilings of a bedchamber and a drawing room. It took time to afford the repair. Once the building was sound, I leased it to a large family whose occupation as painters was put to good use to bring the home back to rights for a reduced rent."

And he'd never looked back. He'd used that experience as a model for his future investments.

Walter shook his head. "I thought you knew. I'll send a note round to the tenant to expect your visit if you still wish to go."

"Thank you," she whispered. "I should like that very much. I had such a happy time visiting my grandparents there as a child."

He nodded in sympathy. She should cling to those happier memories and forget the sad ones. "Now then, Miss Merton, shall we fight for the last helping, or merely toss a coin and let fate decide for us who gets to eat what remains?"

He peered at her with one brow raised and, as hoped, she smiled at his ridiculous suggestion. "I certainly won't fight with such slim odds of success. We all know it is one of your favorites."

They would share, of course. He grinned, served her a modest amount, and placed the remainder on his own plate. "Any dessert is my favorite until I meet the next helping. Don't waste that."

"Has there ever been a battle won over dessert?" Valentine chuckled.

Mrs. Hartwood's eyes widened. "Why, yes, there was, or at least there was in fiction. Over the summer I read this delightful little book. There was just such a scene as you described. Oh, what was that book called?"

There was a scene from a K.L Brahms book that described such an event; however, few knew that Walter was the inspiration for it.

As a boy, he'd been slow to temper and Imogen had often annoyed him with her nattering. At one meal, she'd gone too far over something of no importance. A well-flung spoonful of brandy custard had silenced her until she'd retaliated and they'd gone to war. At first, he'd been amused his sister had remembered a long-ago battle over dessert and had used it in her book.

Until now.

Melanie laughed softly. "That's in *Findings from a Castaway*? From what I can gather, everyone in Brighton has read the story and is talking about what makes the perfect dessert worth fighting over. I don't believe I'd care to have food flung across our dining room, but it makes for a dramatic reading."

"Indeed it does," Mrs. Hartwood said with a shudder. "The scene is described so clearly I can almost see it happening when I close my eyes. Those charming porcelain kittens falling off the mantle and the dollop of custard sliding down that poor girl's cheek."

The girl had been Melanie at age ten or eleven.

Imogen had possessed terrible aim and had been responsible for the broken ornaments. Hitting Melanie had been entirely his fault. Melanie hadn't been expected that day and had been caught by a misaimed shot of his. He winced, remembering her tears over her ruined dress.

Did she remember her part in it? He glanced at her but could detect no recognition in her expression. Perhaps she had forgotten all about it, along with her friendship with Imogen. It *had* been a long time ago.

"Well," Melanie set her napkin aside, "I hope there will be no similar incidents in this house tonight."

Her gaze lingered on him briefly before she turned to Julia. At the subtle rise of her brow, Julia urged Mrs. Hartwood to the parlor for tea, leaving Walter puzzled and eager to know if the family secret was out or not. He truly couldn't accurately gauge Melanie's mood tonight and that meant he'd have to try to find out if she would make trouble for Imogen. He'd have to get her alone again.

He couldn't wait.

Chapter Eight

"We simply must find that darling man a wife, and soon," Mrs. Hartwood gushed as Melanie stirred half a spoonful of sugar into her cup of tea. There was always a point in every evening entertainment when matchmaking came up, so she wasn't surprised. Since the remark was directed at Julia, and not to herself, she kept her mouth closed and her eyes down.

Julia had made a great start on winning over Mrs. Hartwood, a woman who could help her become a fixture in Brighton society one day if she cultivated a friendship with her.

"I do agree," Julia enthused. "Mr. George would make a wonderful husband indeed."

Melanie set her cup aside, waiting, bracing herself for the suggestion that a match be made between her and Walter, since they were so well acquainted. She lifted her gaze slowly.

"I think Miss Langston would be perfect," Mrs. Hartwood suggested.

"There is always Miss Harrow, and of course Miss Enid Vickers has many fine qualities." Julia shook her head. "What do you think, Melanie? You've known Mr. George much longer than I have. Who do you think he should marry?"

That was a question she'd never been able to answer to her own satisfaction and it troubled her now. "I've known him perhaps a year longer on account of my being marginally older than you."

Such a good and amiable man should have married already. Over the past weeks, she'd come to appreciate Walter. He deserved the perfect wife. But now that she had heard the names of other young ladies thrown about as a match for him, she was outraged on his behalf. Those young ladies would never do.

"Well, I have no doubts he's considering making a match now." Mrs. Hartwood beamed. "Did you hear he's given thought to having children? There are not too many gentlemen so obviously meant to be a father as our Mr. George. My grandson's adore his visits, as do many of the young boys living about us. He's always so very tolerant of their requests he join their games, no matter how silly."

Melanie's heart squeezed tight. The moment Walter had spoken of children at dinner, she'd known he was eager for a family of his own. He was always tossing a ball back to some boy or little girl. Kindness was so very easy for him that children adored him. He would be a good father.

When the gentlemen joined them and much teasing ensued between the married couples, she tried not to stare at him. Seated opposite her, Walter seemed so far away. So very different, and yet the more she considered, the more she saw that their interests and attitudes were very similar.

In everything but the one area that would matter so much to him. Children.

Mr. Hartwood approached her and she forced herself to put that unsettling word into its proper place.

"Would you do an old man the honor of a performance on the pianoforte, my dear?" he asked. "I have not heard you play in many months and I am lonely for the sound."

"We all are," Walter agreed quietly.

Valentine and Julia nodded, clearly eager for her to accept and keep their guests happy. "Please play for us," Julia pleaded.

Although she hadn't intended to become the center of attention, she stood. "I should be delighted to."

If she were playing, she might not have to think of Walter with a family of his own. The idea of him kissing another woman unsettled her a great deal. She chose a long piece and commenced to play, losing herself in the melody until the very last notes. When she finished, Mr. Hartwood was satisfied and he and his wife took their leave.

"Do stay where you are, Melanie," Julia gushed. "I do not hear you play enough anymore since we are out so often."

Valentine stood and kissed Julia's cheek. "I'm going to make one last search for that tune I told you about and then it's our turn to play."

She picked another, shorter piece and set about playing. Walter settled in a chair close by and set his hands behind his head. "If I had my way, I'd tear a hole in the wall so I could hear you play more clearly."

Her heart filled with dread at his suggestion. "Valentine plays as well," Melanie reminded him.

"I need to stuff wool in my ears for those times."

Julia huffed. "And here I was thinking you a fair man all night."

He winked at Melanie. "God-awful racket he kicks up. It is so easy to tell the difference."

"You don't mean that," Melanie argued as she fumbled her way through a difficult passage that hadn't troubled her for a long time. A blush was threatening to cover her from head to toe, all from the compliments Walter continued to shower over her and she did not deserve even one. "Valentine plays well. He would be better if he played more often though."

"Not in your league," Walter insisted. "No doubt about that."

Melanie fixed her attention on her sheet music, but she could not seem to perform to her own high standards anymore.

Valentine hurried in, waving a sheet of music in the air. "Here it is, stuck between the covers of another tune."

Melanie drew the piece to a close and stood, keen to allow the married couple free use of the instrument. It was theirs. Her brother and his wife met at the pianoforte and squeezed onto the same stool and Melanie moved to sit and listen.

"They've been looking for that duet all week so they might play together," she explained to Walter.

He rolled his eyes. "This should be torture then."

"Or amusing," she replied, hiding a smile. It could be torture, but she'd suffer the pain if it made the couple happy.

When the playing commenced, she listened for a respectful few minutes, but the pair were making a mess of the passages and talking more than playing. She turned to Walter, unable to remain silent about his surprising purchase. "Thank you for buying my grandmother's house. It looks lovely now."

At first she had thought her father had spent money on the repairs that had brought the house to life again. She couldn't ever pass it without being filled with longing for those happier times. But it was not her father's way to spend more than the minimum sum required on any property he owned. She should have known better than to think so well of him.

He nodded. "The current tenants spend a lot of time in the garden so it's well tended thanks to the horde of children they have."

"A family lives there?"

"Yes, the Clarksons came to Brighton three years ago and have been exceptionally good tenants." He sighed. "If only more were like them."

Clarkson's eldest son had been one of her suitors. "You own other property?"

He nodded. "A dozen houses and shops around Brighton."

Her eyes widened at the number. "But that would make you—"

She glanced away quickly. It would make him a *prize* on the marriage mart. It was a miracle more ladies hadn't set their cap for him on the strength of his wealth alone.

"What?"

"You must be one of the richest men in Brighton," she whispered quietly so her brother did not overhear her remark.

If Walter thought it odd she questioned his finances, he gave no sign. He shrugged. "Not quite. Mr. Hartwood is ahead of me, as is Hawke."

The pianoforte fell silent.

"But you do not act as if you could buy anything you wanted," Julia stated boldly. "You do not dress a dandy nor flaunt your wealth. No one has ever spoken of you in those terms."

Melanie winced. It was one thing to privately assess the assets of a gentlemen, but quite another to have the discussion in a drawing room after a dinner party where the man was a guest.

"Well, that can only be to my advantage." He grinned and seemed entirely unbothered by the discussion. "I must admit I'm not sorry to be spared the fortune hunters seeking me out. I'd much rather be liked for myself than for my money."

"Miss Langston is assuredly after a wealthy husband," Julia warned him.

"You could marry anyone you like," Melanie added in quickly, determined to turn him away from the young lady. Miss Langston wouldn't do for Walter George. Imogen disliked the girl immensely because she did not care to read. That had to be a consideration in his choice.

"That is true." He shrugged again, as if finding the topic boring. "With your dowry, Miss Merton, I'm sure you could have done the same long ago too. We have a lot in common in that respect."

"What about Miss Vickers?" Julia suggested. "She's very pretty."

Valentine burst out laughing. "My word, this is interesting. I've never had a front-row seat to two people matchmaking one poor man. Terribly unfair. I think *he* should have a chance at it, too. Since there is only one unmarried woman in the room, who would you pick for Melanie to marry, Walter?"

"Well, now. That is a serious question."

Her stomach flipped as his attention locked on her. Walter deserved to know her mind before another moment passed, before he suggested something he'd later regret.

She swallowed nervously. "Except I don't wish to marry."

"I'm sure in time you'd grow accustomed to being held," he assured her with a soft smile.

"That is not the reason." She met his gaze. "I don't wish for children, and a husband would expect me to comply."

He blinked and then is eyes widened in surprise.

Beyond him, Julia and Valentine gasped.

"That is absurd. You like children. I've seen you with children," Walter said, stating the obvious.

"Yes, I like other people's children very much, and even more when I hand them back." She smoothed her hands over her skirts, anxiety filling her. "I simply don't wish for my own, I never have, so there is no point in marrying."

He stared into space and Melanie held her breath. His jaw clenched firmly and his brows wrinkled as if he was struggling with a confusing idea.

"Say what is on your mind, sir?"

His face darkened to a deep red and she flinched. Melanie had seen Walter angry only once before. The day Linus Radley had proposed and then insulted her. Walter had been terribly upset with the man. More than he should have been. More than her own brother even.

He was angry now too and she was ashamed to concede she might have led him to think there could be more between them. She'd allowed him to kiss her, and matches had been made on account of far less.

Her heart ached but she couldn't retract her words or change her opinion. She would never put a child through the same despair she'd suffered. She wasn't like other women. Her arms didn't ache to hold a child.

He cleared his throat. "I cannot say what I feel."

"Well I can." Valentine sprang to his feet. "This is something you might have told me. Should have told me long ago."

"I apologize." She bowed her head, contrite but not changed.

"You do realize that despite the distance, our parents expect you to marry very well."

She didn't need the reminder. "They have already been very clear about my duty to the family; they have pressured me to marry for many years with no success. But I am a long way from them so I try not to think about future disagreements."

Walter turned his face aside. If one of Walter's greatest wishes was to have a family, and he'd come to think of her fondly, she must have sorely disappointed him. After a moment, he met her gaze again. "For what reason?"

"I beg your pardon."

"For what reason do you not wish for children." He stared at her hard, clearly baffled by her decision. "Are you afraid to lose your figure?"

Julia gasped and crossed the room to sit at her side. "Mr. George, that is a very rude question you ask."

For a moment, it surprised Melanie to have Julia jump to her defense. Many women in society were vain about their appearance and it pained her that Walter thought so little of her. She didn't care about her figure. Her decision was reasoned, and entirely sensible.

That wasn't much comfort now though. Melanie rubbed her arms. "So, like Mr. Radley, you think maintaining my appearance is all that is important to me."

"Is it the reason?"

She met his gaze steadily. "Of course it is not."

"What will you do? Spend the rest of your life waiting on Julia and her children? Return to Oxford to tend to your parents' ailments in their final years?" Walter asked, his voice rising. "I imagine that will be hard to do convincingly."

"Walter George, that is enough," Julia protested.

"Oh, I don't think so," he snapped.

He leaned forward. "What will happen to you when Julia does not need or want you underfoot anymore? Will your father's estate provide a home for you?"

"Steady on, George," Valentine warned.

Walter rose, towering above her, but she remained seated and held his gaze. She really had upset him over Imogen and she was sorry for that.

"Without her sight, Imogen was prepared to live alone, away from the ones she loved. She couldn't bear the idea of being a burden, of having to be watched and waited on at all times because she could not see the dangers ahead of her."

Melanie shivered. Imogen's illness had once brought on such extreme panic in herself that she had spoken once without thought, venting her fears in a way that made her cringe now. To lose one's sight was a tragedy, but more so in Imogen's case because she wrote such wonderful tales. Melanie had prayed for her recovery every day, but Walter could not know that because she'd done so privately and never breathed a word of it to anyone. All anyone had heard of Melanie was the bad, because her cousin had made everything she said and did seem even worse. "She was very ill."

"She was not ill. She was afraid, and hurt by the things *you* said about her particularly. As was I." His jaw clenched tight a moment. "I thought you'd changed, but you are still entirely selfish. You chose the easy way, to love only yourself. I doubt you could ever put another's needs first."

His accusations stung. She loved many in Brighton, but she had accepted she was not equipped to show it long ago.

She dropped her gaze, thoroughly ashamed of her behavior with Walter. She was exactly the tease to him that Linus Radley had accused her of being.

"I'm sure you are in the right of it. Excuse me." Melanie hurried from the room, running upstairs, away from everyone. She was always a lady, and should never allow anyone to ruffle her feathers, but she couldn't bear Walter's disappointment. He had stripped her of her composure entirely and made her see how he viewed her too.

Her eyes filled with tears as she heard him take his leave abruptly. She had for a brief moment lost what little good sense she possessed but there was no escaping her mistakes. She was not good. Not even Walter believed that of her anymore.

When Julia came to her door a few minutes later, Melanie refused to let her in. She was better off alone. She deserved to be lonely. Telling herself that didn't take away the pain of Walter's anger, though.

Chapter Nine

As much as Melanie longed to remain apart from the household, incessant tapping at her door could not be ignored. Julia had left her largely to her own devices for the past several days, but it appeared her peace was at an end. "Come in, Julia."

The door opened slowly and her sister-in-law smiled at her as if she was wounded. She wasn't—she was broken. Utterly and completely. She didn't know where she'd find the strength to face Walter again.

"I thought you might like some company and perhaps tea," Julia suggested.

She couldn't say no without appearing rude. "Thank you. That would be lovely."

The maid they shared set a tray of tea and biscuits on her dresser and smiled shyly. "Your favorites."

"Thank you, Amy."

"Shall I pour for you both, miss?"

There were two cups on the tray, hinting that Julia intended to remain. "I'm sure we can manage."

The maid glanced around. "I'll just straighten your room a bit."

The room didn't need anything done to it. Melanie had spent the better part of three days here, minding her own business, avoiding her brother and accidental meetings with Walter George. She had straightened everything, even polished a table, but it hadn't made her feel different. She was tired, and she just wanted to be left alone. "There's nothing to be done here. That will be all, Miss Pond, if you don't mind."

The maid appeared crestfallen but then smiled. "Of course. If you need anything, please call for me."

"I will."

Julia closed the door behind the maid with a sigh. "She's worried about you."

"She shouldn't." Melanie crossed the room, poured tea for her sister and passed the cup and a biscuit to her. "Her duty is to you."

Melanie left her cup untouched. "Did you and Valentine enjoy the ball last night?"

"How do you do that? Pretend to feel one thing when you're obviously still upset? You've been hiding in here all week, and don't spout that nonsense again about having a headache."

"I am not upset." She picked up her cup and sipped, hoping Julia did not notice the faint tremble in her hand. She'd been feeling this way for days, on edge and nervous, ever since Walter had insisted she was selfish. "Where is your husband?"

"I sent him out. He went for a long walk."

"I see."

"It's too cold for swimming and the idleness of inactivity is making him edgy. I never knew he was so much like me before."

Melanie smiled. "He used to get into so much trouble at home for rushing through the halls and down the staircases in the mornings. It does him good to be here instead, where he can come and go at will. That reminds me, I have a letter to finish writing to our parents."

She moved to her writing table chair, hoping Julia would take the hint and go. Inside the desk was an incomplete letter to her parents. She was supposed to be heaping praise on Julia for being a good wife. For the first time in her life, she couldn't finish a letter. Julia had surpassed her expectations. However, now that Melanie's secret was out, that she didn't wish to be a wife or mother, she no longer knew what to say to anybody, even in a letter.

She didn't know what to do with herself either, and that was unusual. She should focus on her duty to her family, so she wrenched her mind back to her brother's interests. "At least Valentine's swimming hasn't ever been a bone of contention with the older set. That has always worried me."

Julia perched on the edge of the bed. "He's not the only one who goes."

"True." All his friends went. Walter went.

Melanie kept her gaze on the fine white curtains shrouding the window. She hadn't thrown them wide today. The muted light suited her mood better than the clear day outside. "I would not recommend that you try to join them if you ever want to impress other women."

Julia giggled. "They swim naked, you know."

A blush swept Melanie's cheeks. "The less said about that the better, if you don't mind. I don't like to imagine my brother's friends in that fashion."

"Not even one of them?" Julia discarded her cup and settled herself more fully on the bed, her fingers twisting together in her lap. "I know you say now that you do not wish to marry, but hadn't you set your cap for Hawke not so long ago?"

Melanie frowned at the change of topic. "Anyone could see he was fondest of Abigail."

"And Sir Peter," Julia mused, her brow wrinkling. "Don't you tell me you were not wildly impressed by his title last year?"

"A baronet deserves respect."

Julia, clearly unsatisfied by that answer, jumped to her feet and came closer. "I saw you flirt with him when he came back to Brighton."

Melanie sighed at the memory of that night. "And did you see how well that worked out?"

Julia frowned, her confusion evident. "He asked for Imogen's hand in marriage a second time not long afterward."

Melanie had been relieved by that development. "He did indeed."

"But you couldn't have known he would ask her again."

"His heart always resided there. He just needed another

push—or a fright, as the case was that night—in her direction."

"You flirted with him so he wouldn't consider you? Was that why you were so obvious about it?" Julia slouched untidily, her mouth agape.

She smiled slightly. "Nothing terrifies a man more than a woman who appears hell-bent on marriage."

"Do you know you might just be the most wretchedly devious woman I've ever met?"

She shrugged. "His title, my dowry. Some would have considered that a match made in heaven. Which it would not have been, I assure you. It would not have taken long for some well-meaning person to suggest the match to him, so I made sure the idea was entirely unpalatable to begin with."

Julia grunted. "Teresa said you kept a list of bachelors."

"The list is, *was*, merely an amusement to pass a tedious and dull winter in Oxford while my mother urged me to impress other gentlemen." She eased a folded sheet of paper from between the covers of an older K.L. Brahms book. "I used to try to predict who would make a match before I returned in the summer. I wasn't often wrong."

She passed it to Julia and waited while she read it. It was a single page of neat script. An idle fancy of hers. A gentleman's name, and several potential spouses. Some names had been scratched out, others underlined as she'd settled on her choice for their wife. A few were circled as matches were made.

"Heaven help the man you *do* set your cap for," Julia whispered. "He would have no chance of escape."

Melanie's smile vanished. "I don't want children, so marriage isn't an option for me."

Julia met her gaze. "I've seen you with children, too."

"As I said, I like other people's children but I don't have the temperament for my own."

"How can you be so sure until you have them?"

She thought about her answer a moment. "I can't. But I won't be a willing party to neglect."

"Should I prepare myself for Valentine to be a terrible father to our children?"

"No. My brother will be an exemplary parent."

"So, despite his father being so unfeeling and unsupportive, Valentine will be an exception to his upbringing."

"He already is."

Julia met her gaze. "Then why can't you be too?"

Melanie smiled sadly, unsurprised by Julia's persistence. "You cannot convince me so easily. I have never wanted children of my own."

"I am trying to understand." Julia sighed and then grabbed her hand in a fierce grip. "I think any child would be lucky to have you for a mother. You would be strict, no doubt about that, but you would not be cruel. You would love them and care for them all."

"All?" She shook her head at the idea of having many. She glanced at her trapped hand, and discovered the compulsion to pull back had dimmed a great deal. "Don't trouble yourself over my spinster state. I think the best course of action is to concentrate on you and my brother."

"No more dares." A grin tugged at Julia's lips as she sat back. "Well, not until *after* we've conquered Scafell Pike together next summer."

Melanie dropped her head into her hands. The pair were hell-bent on unconventionality. "Heaven help me."

Julia laughed and then asked the question Melanie had been dreading all week. "Why was Walter George so angry with you?"

Melanie's heart lurched but she'd practiced an answer well. "I suppose the idea of a woman unwilling to have children offended his sensibilities."

"It was more than that."

Melanie bit her tongue, struggling to find a reasonable explanation for Walter's outburst that could satisfy Julia. "He was also defending his sister, as is his right."

"He must have been hiding that anger for a very long time," Julia said, staring at her pointedly. "He's never shown a hint of it before."

She had no answer to that. His emotions had been very high that night. She'd never known his thoughts so clearly until now and still felt the pain of his disappointment. The break in their friendship had been inevitable. "He was entitled to speak his mind, and I did ask him to."

Julia frowned but before she could continue, Valentine burst into the room. "There's been an accident."

Walter.

Heart in her throat, she managed to croak out a steadier question instead. "Who is it?"

"Francis Clemens was struck by a carriage at sunrise. He's dead."

"Oh, poor Jane and the children!" Melanie reeled. Relief that her first fear—that Walter had been hurt—was acute, but now sadness gripped her because she knew the family. She reached for her reticule and found additional handkerchiefs in a nearby drawer. She stuffed them inside. "I must go."

"Do you know them well?" Julia asked.

"They are older acquaintances of mine." Andy's former friends in Brighton. Melanie had continued to seek out the family long after there was a reason. "Good and decent people, but poor. Mr. Clemens's passing will be devastating to his wife. I must pay my respects."

"We'll come with you," Julia volunteered quickly.

"No. Please, if you don't mind, I should like to go alone." She glanced between husband and wife. "Mrs. Clemens is unlikely to wish for strangers to see her and the children on such a terrible day. I will, of course, pass along your condolences."

Valentine nodded. "We will expect your return before dinner."

Melanie struggled into her blue pelisse. "I will do my best not to be too late."

Chapter Ten

"Mr. George, I cannot thank you enough for your generosity," Vicar Pease enthused as they shook hands across his oak desk.

"Think nothing of it." Walter set his hat to his head, eager to be on his way to make preparations for moving the Clemens widow and children into their new home since they were set to be evicted by day's end. It had been a devastating week for them.

With Clemens gone and no surety of income ahead, their landlord had given the widow notice she'd be evicted by today. He'd been horrified when he'd learned of it this morning. "I am happy to help a family in need. If all goes well, Mrs. Clemens should be settled in her new home in a few hours. I had planned visiting her myself and passing along the news. But would you care to visit her new home with me now? I'm on my way there directly."

"I think that's a fine idea. I will meet you outside in a moment." The vicar tugged on his coat. "I'll just inform my wife that I'm going out."

The vicar stepped from the room and Walter strolled out to the street frontage, taking a moment to glance around him.

Unfortunately, his gaze caught on Melanie Merton a moment later.

They had not spoken for a week by his design, but he'd not

needed to expend much effort to avoid her. According to Julia, she'd largely kept to the house.

He hadn't wanted to see her. He'd been moments away from humiliating himself by suggesting himself as her husband. When she'd revealed the extent of her indifference to men and marriage and children, he'd lost his temper entirely because it made no sense.

She hurried toward him now though, a determined expression on her pale face. He was surprised to see she was alone, when she'd always been so particular about her maid accompanying her everywhere in the past. He prepared himself to be polite as she drew near. "Miss Merton."

"Mr. George." She glanced about, her gaze lingering on the vicar's front door. "What an unexpected surprise to see you here."

"I am waiting on the vicar to join me."

Her shoulders sank and she glanced past him. "I wished to speak to him too."

"I expect him at any moment."

True to his word, Pease bowled out of the front door and rushed to his side. The vicar flicked his hand from side to side. "I've no time to speak to you today."

"But I only wanted to enquire about aid for Mrs. Clemens," she rushed to say before the man could move past her. "She has nowhere to go."

A disapproving expression crossed the vicar's face. "We are seeing to that now. She has been taken care of. Shall we go, Mr. George?"

The rude snub startled Walter. Melanie might not have the stomach for the ill and injured, but he was touched that she asked after a poor blacksmith's widow. The family should have been quite beneath her. "We are just seeing her settled into a new abode now."

She met his gaze warily. "I am pleased to hear it, especially with winter not far off. Might I ask where she will live?"

The vicar cleared his throat. "Mr. George, did you not say you were in somewhat of a hurry?"

"Not so much as to be rude to Miss Merton." He gave her the directions. "Would you care to accompany us?"

He expected her to decline.

"Thank you. I should like to see the place for myself so I might find it later." She nodded and they walked side by side along the cobblestone streets toward the small home he would offer the widow. It was a relatively new purchase, and the broken windowpanes had been replaced only yesterday. All it should require was a thorough sweeping out before Mrs. Clemens and her brood could move in.

Vicar Pease filled the silence with talk of business and entertainments, but largely ignored Melanie. Walter, on the other hand, could not. They had argued; or rather, he had finally spoken from his heart about how her behavior had affected him. He felt awkward around her now and foolish. Walter never liked to let resentments linger. She would not change and he should not have expected it. The fact he was disappointed she wouldn't marry anyone, even him, was entirely his mistake. Unfortunately, with the Vicar nearby, he could not speak of the matter candidly.

When the small home he'd offered to Mrs. Clemens came into view, he pointed it out to her. "There. I hope it will be large enough."

Melanie squinted at it, her eyes assessing. "It seems on the small side."

Walter nodded, agreeing with her. "The home had two bedchambers upstairs and none below. For a family of eleven it will be quite a squeeze, but there is nothing else available in Brighton, nothing else offered to the family. It is the best that can be done at short notice."

Mr. Pease shook his head, casting another disapproving glance at Melanie. "Of course it will be large enough and Mrs. Clemens will be grateful, as we all should for another's charity to those in need."

Walter couldn't miss the sharpness of his tone, and fumed. He addressed his reply to the vicar. "Believe me, if I had a bigger home that was unoccupied, I would have offered that instead and not have the worry of whether everyone would fit inside. Mr. Clemens was well known to my father, and a good man he was too."

He caught Melanie's elbow out of habit and guided her up the short flight of stairs ahead of the vicar before he realized what he was doing. He was supposed to be angry with her, but in the face of such rudeness, he couldn't seem to suppress his protective instincts around her.

He dropped her arm at the door when he realized she hadn't eased away from him on her own. She remained close enough that, when he inhaled, the jasmine perfume she often wore filled his lungs. It was a pleasant scent. A subtle fragrance he'd always associated with the woman.

Much like the knowledge that she would only marry a man who'd made something of himself.

Except that wasn't to be either.

He steeled his heart against that disappointment and unlocked the house using his key.

Inside, the property was a good deal cooler than outside. He kept his hat in his hands and overcoat on to ward off the chill. Melanie, dressed in a light wool coat, rubbed her arms briskly while she inspected the lower floor of the property and then disappeared upstairs, clutching her garments around her as if she were chilled through.

She'll need a thicker coat for winter.

"What am I doing?" he muttered to himself. He glanced down. *For heaven's sake, the woman can take care of herself. She doesn't even want a man in her life; much less have me fussing over her. Let it go!*

He nodded and then checked the quality of work on the rear windows. By the time he was done with his inspection, so was she.

Her firm nod of approval brought relief. "They'll manage well enough here. Have the chimney's been swept in recent time? A good fire will warm up the space enough that they will be very cozy indeed."

He glanced around. "That is what I hoped for too, so the sweeps were here last week."

She stopped at his side, a little behind him, as the vicar approached. "Well, this is quite a fine house for the widow until she remarries," the vicar enthused.

"I doubt she will ever remarry. Mrs. Clemens loved her

husband dearly and keenly feels his loss." He expected the family to need support for some time to come, at least until the elder children found work. "It will suit for the winter and then in the spring, we will see what else can be done."

He gestured for Melanie to precede him from the house and she hurried away from the vicar and his dark scowls.

The vicar held him back when he would have followed. "I do not like the way that woman constantly sticks her nose where it is not wanted."

Melanie's interest in those less fortunate than herself was one of the few things Walter had always liked about her. Despite her haughtiness, she was always very willing to show kindness to widows and children. More than one little girl in Brighton wore a pretty new smock embellished with Melanie's stitches. He couldn't understand why she would not want to have her own offspring to spoil. "Is that so?"

"Indeed. She's hardly the sort to set a good example, the way she taunts proper gentlemen." The vicar glanced toward the door. "She should be minding a husband's concerns by her age."

"Pease!" Walter warned in a low voice. "You are aware that Miss Merton is my neighbor, and my friend's sister, are you not?"

"Yes, well, I don't doubt that places you at a disadvantage." Pease grimaced. "But a man must be free to speak his mind. I'm sure it will be impossible to send her away."

"Indeed it would be, since I have no wish to do so. Any gossip you may have heard of her is completely false and a product of a small minded and petty individual I assure you." Walter scowled and ushered him to the door so he could lock the house. "Do not feel you must accompany us to see Mrs. Clemens. Good day, sir."

He strolled to Melanie, wrapped her arm about his, and steered her away from the man. "Mr. Pease will not be joining us."

She peered over her shoulder. "He does not approve of me."

"You heard."

She sighed and put a distance between them. "It is impossible *not* to hear someone used to delivering sermons and every other word at the top of his lungs. You've no need to speak up for me, or accompany me to see Mrs. Clemens. I can go alone."

"Impossible. I was going to see her now myself. We might as well walk there together." He glanced over his shoulder. Assured they'd left the odious man behind, Walter slowed his pace. "I didn't realize you were acquainted with Mrs. Clemens."

"She was Andy's friend. We used to visit her when I was a girl." Melanie worried at her lip. "We've never moved in the same circles, of course, but after Andy died, every Christmas and at Easter, I have made something new for Mrs. Clemens and her girls."

"I see," he murmured. He was touched she'd been so generous to an old friend of her governess's. "Once Mrs. Clemens is settled in her new home, I must broach the subject of her children's futures with her, but perhaps you know the family better than I and could offer advice."

"There are so many." An odd catch in her voice when she spoke of the children made him wonder if she ever regretted her decision about not having her own.

"Mr. Clemens was devoted to his wife and she was devoted to him. With such affection, it is inevitable that an abundance of children would follow," he murmured.

"I've been to visit her several times since the accident." She glanced up at him. "The elder pair of children might suit as a maid or footman if only they were a little older."

The elder girl was also very pretty, and could easily end up in the wrong sort of company if her mother didn't keep a watchful eye. "I thought so too. Unfortunately, I don't know of anyone in need of a maid or footman so young at the moment."

"Julia does." Melanie frowned. "Or perhaps it would be correct to say I could need a new servant. My maid now tends to Julia first."

"That is a very good suggestion. I will speak to Valentine about it tonight."

"You cannot. I fear Mrs. Clemens would be upset if her eldest child was taken into employment so soon after losing her husband. She quite relies on the girl."

Economics demanded someone in the family had to find employment, and soon. "At your brother's house, she will not be so far away as to trouble Mrs. Clemens's heart, and if there was still concern, perhaps she would be reassured if the girl tended to you instead of Julia."

"It might work if circumstances were different." She turned her face away. "I have been thinking it might be better for Valentine and Julia if I wasn't living with them."

"Where would you go?" He stopped Melanie outside Mrs. Clemens's residence and stared into a face grown even paler than when he'd first seen her that day.

"I am reconsidering my decision to remain in Brighton. Perhaps it would be best if I return to my parents before the festive season is upon us."

He was stunned. "But I thought that business of you leaving was forgotten?"

"I have come to believe you were correct. I am not needed here." She hurried to the weather-beaten door and rapped sharply on it before he could refute her words.

She *was* needed. She was *wanted*.

A boy of about twelve met them and ushered them into a shabby front room. "Miss Merton is here again, Mama."

Mrs. Clemens sat with her youngest child on her knee, staring into a cold hearth. She blinked and looked around. When she made to rise and greet them, Melanie quickly urged her to remain seated and took a place at her side. "Mr. George has come with good news for you."

The babe Mrs. Clemens held reached for Melanie, and to his surprise, she perched the child on her lap as if she were accustomed to it. He tore his gaze away as she fussed, rewrapping the child in a blanket to keep him warm. There was a definite chill in the room. Apparently his help couldn't come too soon.

He cleared his throat. "Yes, indeed. I have a house to offer you on Russell Road. It might be a bit cramped at first, but should do well enough for the winter."

Mrs. Clemens nodded, and then shook her head as if she couldn't believe what she was hearing.

Melanie juggled the child to grasp the woman's hand. "It is true. You have a home again."

Mrs. Clemens topped sideways onto Melanie's shoulder and sobbed, great gasping tears that brought her children running into the room. Melanie put her arm around the woman. "Children, would you take young Vincent and see if you cannot find his rattle? Your mother needs a moment."

The eldest girl took her brother with a smile and dragged her brothers and sisters with her. Melanie squeezed Mrs. Clemens as if they were old friends. "They always listen to Beatrice, don't they?"

Mrs. Clemens turned her head toward Melanie. "I don't know what I would do without her."

"Well, thanks to Mr. George's generosity, you'll never need to find out." She cast a warm smile in his direction and then dug a fine white handkerchief from her reticule to dab away the woman's tears. "Now, would you like to hear about your new home? It is clean and vacant and you will be able to move there today."

Walter filled Mrs. Clemens's ears with the particulars of the property, the nearest neighbors, while also stressing it would be a bit of a squeeze. He stood and checked the time on his pocket watch. "I have arranged for four fellows to lend a hand with the heavy lifting if that is acceptable to you. Honest and trustworthy men who will take care of everything you require done and give you no cause for concern. They should be here directly. This is your key."

The woman grasped it tightly to her chest. "I don't know how I can ever repay you."

He smiled at her warmly. "Some of my happiest memories are of hearing Mr. Clemens sing in the tavern, and I was very sorry to hear of his death. To do any less for his widow would be to slight those happy memories."

Her eyes welled with tears again. "He had a fine singing voice."

"He did indeed."

While Melanie said her goodbyes, Walter silently observed her. Today she'd discarded her reserve in order to comfort the grieving widow. She was good with children, and although it wasn't his place—or wise—a compulsion to explain something to her that would be positively shocking stirred in him.

Avoiding children did not mean she must not marry.

Melanie was making a mistake in denying herself the chance to be happy, and she was clearly unaware of the alternatives.

Chapter Eleven

* * *

With the matter of moving Mrs. Clemens into her new home underway, Melanie allowed herself a moment to relax. "You are a good man, Mr. George."

And generous. She'd had trouble hiding her astonishment at his offer of a home for the family earlier, and later again in the arrangements he'd made for moving them there. He'd also ensured they'd have food on the table and in the pantry. She couldn't imagine another soul being so generous without expecting something in return.

"Don't sound so surprised," he said quietly.

His tone was very much like the Walter she'd always met with in the past—self-deprecating and calm—and her nerves settled. She was sorry circumstances prevented them from being on good terms all the time.

He sighed. "Now, we have the walk home for privacy, so tell me what you did to put the vicar's nose so far out of joint that he would be openly rude to you."

To explain would remind Walter of the reason for their quarrel, and while she did not want to fight with him, she also could not ignore his request. "He feels I set a bad example by not having married yet, and I suppose he is right."

Walter rubbed his jaw in that way he usually did when he was thinking. "You have turned down your fair share of suitors, so it's bound to draw criticism."

She stiffened.

He nodded politely to an acquaintance they passed. "Not that I don't now have some idea why you refused them."

"You don't understand." He certainly hadn't the other day, and she didn't expect that to change. No one understood. Even Valentine looked at her as if she were a stranger.

"I believe I do in a way." He frowned. "Your former suitors failed to make you care for them. You never considered any other response."

His words chilled her. "Are you trying to say that I'm incapable of deeper feelings?"

Walter shook his head. "If you had liked them, or thought you could learn to love even one of those fellows, given a longer acquaintance, your answers might have been different. I suppose from your point of view, you did them a kindness."

She faced forward, feeling her face heating all over again. He *did* understand. "There is no point in marrying only to be miserable. I have witnessed that firsthand through my parents' marriage."

"Not all marriages are bad ones and you are certainly capable of deeper feelings," he continued. "You've grown to love Julia as a sister—and we both know you enjoyed being kissed so, clearly, you are not unaffected if approached the right way."

"That was…" She swallowed. "You caught me by surprise but I should not have allowed it. I am truly sorry."

His eyelids lowered, and a tiny smile appeared on his lips. "I gave you plenty of time to get away."

She couldn't protest it wasn't true. She'd had ample time and opportunity to avoid the second kiss he'd pressed to her lips. She couldn't explain why she hadn't moved but the idea of turning him away hadn't once crossed her mind. It wasn't until after the kiss that she'd realized what she'd done. She'd led him on unintentionally.

He leaned close. "As much as I'd like to discuss kissing, I have something else on my mind today that I want to talk to you about."

Melanie clenched her hands together, overcome by fear of what else he might have to say of her past behavior.

She waited for him to continue but he kept glancing toward the sea. "Walter?"

His brows lifted and then he glanced down. "This is a public area, and I'm not one to harm a lady's reputation. There is something I need to explain to you that is difficult to say but I feel I must."

"All right. If you think it's important, I shall hear you."

"I want you to understand that while I might not accept your decision not to marry, I don't deny you the right not to. I apologize if I was short with you last week. I'd like to hope we could remain on good terms irrespective of what I say next."

A rush of yearning filled her. The past week had been painful, thinking that she'd angered him, disappointed him. She'd had sufficient time to consider how she might mend their friendship, but until today she'd begun to feel it a lost cause. "I'd like that."

He took a deep breath. "A woman need not suffer a pregnancy if she does not want a babe. There are ways to avoid such a situation."

That hadn't been what she'd expected to hear next from him. "I don't understand."

"I can see that you don't." He stared ahead, his cheeks darkening to a deep pink, as if he were blushing. "A husband can withdraw from his wife before he finds completion during intimacy. You could marry if you wanted to and still not have children."

Melanie swallowed hard. She'd never known such things were possible in a marriage. She'd never been told very much about a wedding night except to expect pain and repetition until a child was made. "No husband would agree to such an arrangement that denied him an heir."

"He might accept if given a choice in the decision from the beginning."

"No man would want society to think he'd chosen so poorly. A supposedly barren wife would be an embarrassment to him."

"Then he would be a buffoon," Walter insisted. He met her gaze. "There is no need to deny yourself the pleasure of intimacy. There are more ways and means for a husband to be with his wife without causing a babe to be made."

Melanie gasped. "There are?"

He stared at her and his face turned very red. "Oh, yes."

She set her hand to her throat as embarrassment filled her. This was a side to Walter George that she'd never suspected. He was a wolf in sheep's clothing!

What he suggested bordered on the scandalous, and she should not listen to another word.

She hurried ahead of him but when she reached the end of the lane, she slowed her steps. What exactly was she running from? He spoke of her taking a husband as if she had choices when she knew there were none.

He caught up to her quickly. "Does that change your mind?"

She considered what answer to give. She couldn't say yes or even no with any certainty. She had only a little understanding of what went on between husbands and wives in the bedchamber. Where Walter had gotten his experience and knowledge of intimacy was a subject she didn't want to contemplate. "I don't know."

"That's not a no." His small smile grew and they continued on in silence a few more yards. "Perhaps practical experience of desire might help you decide whether to give up entirely on men."

She frowned at his suggestion. She had to assume he intended to be her teacher on the subject. She *had* enjoyed his kisses, but no self-respecting lady would agree with him. "I can't."

"No expectations, no consequences. Be honest with me now, could you think of anything when we were kissing?"

"I. Ah. No." She met Mr. George's gaze guiltily. That was what had set them at odds in the first place. Her lack of restraint. Her lack of caution around him. "I didn't think of very much at all."

He grinned. "Tomorrow, after your brother and Julia head off to the shop, give your servants the day off. Tell them you want to read all day or something equally unexciting. When they are gone, I will come to you. Leave the front door unlocked so I can slip inside before anyone sees me."

She stared at him in horror. "Have you done this before with other women?"

He grinned. "Does the idea of me with someone else make you uncomfortable?"

"Yes," she replied immediately. It made her seethe. "I thought you were a respectable gentlemen."

"There are degrees to everything, and I won't pretend I don't want you."

She blushed at his bold statement. To think she'd been so comfortable around a rogue and not known his true colors. "I couldn't do what you ask."

He huffed out a breath. "Damn. I almost had you there for a moment."

When he laughed and threw his usual smile her way, she was confused. It was as if he'd become two very different men all of a sudden. She liked one of them. She wasn't so certain about the other.

They walked home in silence and he made no further advances. She was surprised he was taking her rejection so well.

She stole a glance at him and he caught her looking. "If you ever change your mind, you know where to find me," he whispered.

They met Valentine at the end of Cavendish Place and her brother's face was so pale, she gasped. "What's wrong?"

"What's wrong," Valentine hissed. "Where the devil have you been?"

Astonished by his anger, she swallowed the lump in her throat. "I went to enquire after Mrs. Clemens's situation and ended up helping her move into the new home Mr. George has provided for her."

"I will bid you both a good evening," Walter said before abandoning her to her brother's interrogation. She felt a pang of longing to follow him, but quickly quashed that idea.

"Have you no care for your reputation anymore?" Valentine scowled. "You left without taking your maid along and now I see you've met with Walter. What did he say to you this time to make your face blush so?"

"Amy was busy helping Julia sort the linen today and I didn't want to disturb their plans." She gestured toward Walter as he let himself into his home and disappeared inside. "Mr. George was perfectly amiable, so there was no cause for any concern."

She turned for the front door of their home, wishing desperately to vanish instead. Julia smiled warmly when they met inside, but Melanie sidestepped her sister-in-law and headed to her bedchamber. Despite his shocking suggestion and advances, Walter had given her much to consider. Whatever these methods of avoiding conception were, she'd never heard a whisper of them.

Valentine poked his head through her doorway. "I begin to wonder what is going on between you two. First he yells at you and now you call him amiable!"

"There is nothing between us," she insisted. There should never be.

He nodded. "See to it that there can never be any misunderstandings. He is too good a friend to lose. We owe him a great deal."

"I know." She glanced at her brother. "I don't wish another misunderstanding either, not with the way Mr. Radley reacted."

Valentine turned away.

"Wait," she called out to him. "We should discuss when I could return to our parents."

"Never." Valentine reappeared at the doorway. "Why on earth would you want to go back to them?"

Melanie shook her head. "We never spoke of it, but my stay should have only ever been a temporary tactic to divert Father's temper. With Mrs. Hartwood's support for Julia assured, and her doing so well, it is high time I got out from underfoot."

"I did not mean to make you feel uncomfortable. I am trying to understand your decision, truly I am, but you must know how strange it is for me. I'd always assumed you were waiting for the right gentlemen to ask for your hand."

"I do understand how strange my decision must seem to you." She shrugged. "I tried to tell you once before, but you laughed and turned away without realizing I was in earnest. I lost my courage then. It is time I went home."

"This is your home," Valentine insisted.

"No, it is Julia's, and I promise you I am happy for that." She smiled at him, but could see he was torn. "Could you please make arrangements for a carriage, or I can take the stage on my own if that is more convenient and thrifty. I don't wish to be a burden to you."

Taking the stage on Friday would allow her time to say goodbye to Mrs. Clemens and to Walter.

Valentine sighed, raking his fingers through his hair. "A private carriage and a suitable chaperone, as always. I won't have you placed in any danger, and I expect you to return for the summer each year without fail."

"If you insist." Melanie would not come again. It was time to let go of the past and this place. She grasped the door and slowly shut it in his face.

However, she trembled so badly, she climbed onto her bed and grasped the small pillow to hug against her chest. She was being torn in two by conflicting desires.

She wanted to stay with all her heart, but Walter would always yearn for children and the idea he'd have them with someone else caused her more pain than she'd ever imagined possible. She hadn't felt this wretched since Andy had passed away.

Chapter Twelve

The obligations of meeting expectations, even if it were to his married sister on her birthday, were becoming a trial. This extravagant dinner could not be over soon enough for Walter's taste. He kept his eyes on his plate, a smile on his lips and ignored the subtle flirtations aimed at him from his left.

"Have you traveled much, Mr. George?"

Walter was hard pressed not to groan each time Miss Lane opened her mouth. She was determined to make him notice her. He glanced along the table and regretted Melanie's absence from the festivities. If only she had come, he would not be the target of a marriage-minded miss. "Yes, I've traveled all over, but I prefer Brighton."

"And London, I hope." The woman giggled and glanced across to her parents. The family lived most of the year in London, from what he could tell, and it was becoming blatantly obvious where she was attempting to lead the discussion. If he hinted he visited the capital on occasion then an invitation to call on them would undoubtedly be extended.

He shrugged. "I've no need for London."

Given the strength of the sigh that followed, Walter assumed the girl was disappointed in him but he didn't care.

He was the only single man at this dinner. Miss Lane the only one unmarried. He was highly sick of the matchmaking attempts. Soon, if he had his way, he would not have to endure such indignities.

He knew his own mind.

He was decided on Melanie for a wife, and no amount of flirtatious looks from young Miss Lane would ever persuade him to give up what he wanted so easily. It would take time, but he was sure he could change her mind. She'd changed it once to allow him to kiss her, and the rest would surely come eventually if he did not rush her into a situation that went against her morals.

Luckily he was possessed with abundant patience.

The meal ended and, to his relief, the women filed out for the drawing room soon after. Miss Lane threw a swift smile over her shoulder as she stepped across the threshold. Although it was his brother-in-law's duty, Walter stood immediately to serve port. He needed the drink to brace himself for what remained of the evening.

Peter sidled up to him. "What did you think of Miss Lane?"

He tossed back the contents of his glass and continued pouring for everyone else. "What's to consider?"

He shared the glasses around and then made himself comfortable for some peace, quiet and preferably masculine conversation.

Miss Lane's father, now with port in hand, raised it in a toast. "To the ladies."

"To our ladies," Peter murmured before setting his glass aside.

Mr. Lane thought himself something of a poet, and knowing he had a captive audience, began to quote his work out loud. Walter's friends clapped respectfully and then turned the conversation to local events. He was praised for his assistance to Mrs. Clemens then Peter leaned close. "I must warn you. If you have not noticed, the ladies have it in their heads to find you a wife."

Walter paused with his drink halfway to his lips. "That would be a mistake."

"Imogen thought so too at first, but I fear Mrs. Hawke and Mrs. Merton have convinced her you just need to meet the right woman."

He'd met her when he was ten years old. He took a long sip of his drink and shook his head at the astonishing idea.

He glanced across at Valentine Merton, noting the man was deep in his own thoughts again. Valentine had been that way all night and he was puzzled by it. Even Julia had been quiet enough during dinner to make him concerned. Was something wrong between the newlyweds again?

Walter moved toward Valentine. "What's the matter?"

The man considered his answer a long time before he said, "My sister wants to leave Brighton."

"She might have mentioned something of that nature in passing, I think." He'd not believed her serious about it though.

Valentine sipped his port then grimaced. "She set a date. Friday."

Walter was left reeling by the news he only had two more days to see her. "You couldn't change her mind?"

"I've never been very good at that." He raked his fingers through his hair. "She's like a dog with a bone when she makes a decision. Even more so when I don't like it."

"I see."

Stubborn woman. Her mind had to change or they'd both be miserable alone.

He accepted another drink as he pondered how convincing her to stay might be accomplished. Short of compromising her, he was left with kidnapping and imprisonment as his only other option.

Mr. Lane returned and droned on for a while about his latest project but when it was time to rejoin the ladies, Walter made his excuses and fled the party. Rather than go home, he headed for the seashore to do some serious thinking. Spending the night hours by the water was a particular favorite, even if one always had to keep an eye open for any unscrupulous scoundrels who preyed on the weak and unmindful.

He halted at the edge of the grass, unwilling to ruin his best boots in saltwater and sand, and absorbed the view. Moonlight shone silver upon the restless channel, lighting up the night and the incoming tide. There was always something to see on the shore and tonight was no exception. How could Mellie think to leave all this beauty again?

Ahead of him, a deep shadow marked debris left behind by earlier waves and he peered at it curiously. Once, he'd discovered a satchel of women's clothing and had concluded it part of a cargo lost from a passing ship.

The shape on the beach grew in size however and he stared, and then laughed at his folly. Judging by the shape, a woman, long skirts clinging to her legs, had allowed the sea to claim her attention a touch too long and now suffered the consequences of being waterlogged. She was struggling to walk.

He hurried to offer aid, skidding down the slope haphazardly in his haste. She drew back, glancing left and right, her arms outstretched to keep him back.

"Don't be alarmed," he said quickly. "I only wished to give you the aid of my arm."

"Walter?" Melanie exclaimed. "Oh, you scared me half to death!"

"Mellie?" He glanced left and right too, searching for Melanie's maid, and failed to find any sign of the woman, or indeed any other person nearby. He rushed to her side. "What the devil do you think you are doing out here alone?"

"Attempting to gather shells to take home with me," She glanced around her. "I remember seeing some here this afternoon but they are gone now."

"Your brother will skin you alive."

She trudged past him, hands fisted into her skirts. "He will say nothing."

"Like hell he will," Walter grumbled as he followed her.

"My brother believes I am at home." Melanie stopped a little farther up the beach and paused to make a futile attempt to wring out seawater from the bottom of her gown. "I would appreciate it if you could keep our meeting here tonight between us."

A breaking wave surged toward them and Walter swung her up into his arms to carry her away from danger.

She struggled the entire way. "Unhand me!"

He pulled her tighter against his chest. "By the time you make it off the beach, the bottom of your skirts, your footwear and stockings will be beyond salvation. Stop fighting me and I'll have you sorted out in a moment. At the rate we are moving, anyone could see us together and I don't care to contemplate the assumptions they will make."

The township would question her virtue if she were caught alone with him on a night like this. During the day was one thing if they were simply walking side by side, but out at night—everyone would get the wrong idea.

She ceased her struggles and he set her atop the grassy slope gently. Her skirts slapped wetly as he released her legs and he caught a handful of the sodden garment and squeezed out as much seawater as he could manage. "You should not be out at night alone," he scolded and then urged her toward home. "Anything could have happened to you."

She shrugged. "I do thank you for your help. A wave caught me unawares."

"You must know it is dangerous for you to be out alone."

"It is dangerous for a woman anywhere. Even stepping onto a terrace for a breath of cool air can place her reputation in jeopardy."

"So being caught kissing you would not be in your best interests."

She sighed. "My brother would be very angry with me if he ever found out I'd allowed you to."

"Still, it is an enjoyable pastime. Kissing you," he clarified.

She shifted subtly away from him, and shivered. Walter quickly tore off his coat and wrapped her in the heavy wool without asking her leave. "You need to wear a thicker coat at this time of year."

She shrugged again.

He leaned into her a little. "When I saw you on the beach, I thought I'd found another bit of lost property."

She hugged his coat tighter around her and struggled on. "As apt a description as any."

"You were not at Imogen's birthday dinner tonight."

Mellie sighed. "No."

"Why not?"

"I was not invited," she whispered softly.

That startled him. In times past, no matter what might be

preferred, Melanie had never been excluded from an entertainment. His own sister delivered the most stinging cut. It would be noticed, remarked upon, questioned.

When he married Melanie, he would have to do something about Imogen so future snubs did not occur. He had not revealed to Imogen the details of Andy's death yet, and how Melanie had suffered such a terrible shock at a young age. But he might have to. It could soften the friction between the two women so peace was restored.

"I'm sorry." He put his arm around Melanie and briskly rubbed her arm. "I could have done with your company tonight."

"You did not enjoy dining with Mr. Lane, his wife and daughter?"

Dear God, of course she would know who would be in attendance. There were few secrets in Brighton kept longer than a day. "Mr. Lane likes the sound of his own voice very much. Miss Lane chatters. Sets a man's teeth on edge. I had little conversation with the mother. They are likely still at Imogen and Peter's. I left as soon as I possibly could."

She glanced at him swiftly then glanced away again. "She's a lovely young woman. Very accomplished."

"To someone else's standards perhaps."

She said nothing to that.

"Every man has them, you know." He laughed to himself. He had very high standards indeed. He didn't think there was another woman to match them but the woman at his side. "But it doesn't do to mention them out loud or other people start making plans for your future."

She shrugged off his coat and pushed it toward him. "I am warmer now. You should put this back on before you catch a chill yourself."

"And I had best see you safely home."

"I can find my own way," she said quickly, attempting to dismiss his protection.

He slipped her arm though his as soon as he'd donned his coat. "Good, because quite frankly, I might be lost without you."

She did not laugh at his attempt at humor. In fact, she appeared downright suspicious of his claim. As much as he'd like to explain further, he had to return her home. He'd already taken too many risks with her reputation as it was, although he did not exactly regret parts of their interactions.

With dryer skirts, Melanie was able to move swiftly. Once they'd reached the well-trod path, she hurried forward without looking back. It was as if…

He sprinted after her and blocked her way. "What's wrong?"

"Please, just leave me be," she begged.

He was taken aback by her wail, so unlike her usual calm demeanor that he was concerned. "Not until you tell me what's changed. I thought we had settled our differences."

"I can't ever be what you want." She wrung her hands. "You know I won't, so if you are after female companionship, you should look elsewhere."

He grabbed her arm and felt the tremble in her limb. "What the devil has gotten into you to speak this way?"

She stared up at him, eyes wide in the moonlight. "I promised Valentine I wouldn't encourage you, and I don't mean to."

Walter gaped. Valentine was scolding the wrong party in this affair. He cupped the back of Melanie's head and drew her against his chest in a clumsy embrace. "I could hardly be disappointed. I only want you to be happy and you are not. I enjoy our time together too much to risk losing you. I felt it necessary to set you straight about avoiding conception and overstepped. I am sorry if I made you uncomfortable. I won't even kiss you if you say you don't want me to."

He held his breath.

She met his gaze sadly and turned away. "Good night, Mr. George."

"Wait, I will need the name of a comfortable inn in Oxford."

She faced him again. "Why would you want that?"

"Because if you're leaving Brighton on Friday, I'm going to follow you there."

"You can't do that!"

"As you discovered last week, I am wealthy enough to do anything I want. You certainly couldn't imagine I'd want to stay behind this time. If you go, I'll be moving to Oxford, temporarily I hope, so I can claim my favorite dance partner and talk to you again."

He'd ruined his chances of a slow courtship by speaking precipitously of intimacy before she was ready, but he wasn't going to let the obstacle of distance deter him.

He bent to press a gentle kiss her cheek. "I'll see you in the morning, and every morning after that no matter what you say."

"Walter, you can't mean that."

"But I do." He met her gaze. "Moving will not keep us apart, so just give up and stay. Agreed?"

She stared at him so long his heart began to thump against his ribs. He drew a breath, willing her to find her courage—and then he jumped as a servant from her home stepped outside. They were undoubtedly spotted. Thankfully it was only her maid.

She licked her lips. "You'll come to hate me."

"I don't think that's possible." He caught her elbow and urged her toward her maid. "Take your mistress inside and make sure she is warmed as soon as possible."

"Yes, sir." The maid grinned. "Not a word about this, I suppose?"

"My thanks." He kissed the back of Melanie's glove and then left her, grinning ear to ear. He could change her mind eventually. He was sure of it.

Chapter Thirteen

"Melanie, we need you in the parlor," Julia called from the hallway outside her closed bedroom door.

Melanie set the last of her packing into the trunk and closed the lid. After all the years she'd spent in Brighton, she was having trouble reducing her possessions to a reasonable amount for travel. She was going home, despite Walter's plea to stay. Leaving Brighton behind for the regulated life of a daughter who could never make her parents happy was a small price to pay for peace of mind.

After a night spent contemplating her feelings, she understood she had fallen in love with Walter George.

She just couldn't figure out *when* it had happened.

Not that she could or should do anything about her feelings. He wanted children and she still did not. She couldn't deny him what he wanted most, so that meant going ahead with her original plan on Friday without telling him what she was doing.

She dragged her feet to the doorway and then squared her shoulders. Time to pretend she was happy about leaving in the face of Julia's mournful expression.

Dearest Julia just didn't understand how painful living here would be after Walter had given up on her. Even the idea of him with other women in her imagination was painful.

She made her way downstairs and stopped short in the parlor doorway. Julia hadn't shared her plans for the day so she was surprised to find the room was full. Her stomach flipped. "Lady Watson, Mrs. Hawke. What an unexpected pleasure."

Many months large with child, Abigail Hawke waddled across the room to kiss her cheek in greeting. Her rounded stomach bumped her. "It's good to see you again."

The small dog she owned bounced around them, paws raised as if eager to say hello too. Melanie bent to pat its head, knowing the animal would continue pleading for attention if ignored. "I had not heard of your arrival."

Abigail squeezed her hand. "We arrived from London very late last night. Hawke surprised me with this trip so I had no time to send a letter ahead to announce we were coming. He has some great secret he will not share no matter how much I plead with him."

"A matter concerning your husband's bank?"

Abigail frowned. "No, I do not think that is his business that brings us. Mr. Knight and the new partner, Lord Beecroft, are involved though. They would not answer my questions either so it remains a surprise. I am terribly intrigued."

Melanie nodded but dismissed the matter. She glanced at Julia. "You said you needed me?"

"Not me," Julia said quickly.

Abigail twisted to look at Imogen. "It is not us who drags you to the parlor, but Lady Watson."

"Oh." Melanie glanced between the ladies. Julia practically bounced in her seat, Abigail beamed and Imogen sat impassively, regarding her curiously but without the faintest trace of warmth in her expression. "What is it I need to hear?"

Silence lengthened and Imogen's brow rose.

"Am I supposed to guess?"

"I suppose not." Her lips pressed together tightly a moment. "Julia insisted I tell you myself. I am with child."

Melanie froze but then tears filled her eyes at the hard way Imogen delivered her news. The thin edge of hostility reminded her that no matter what she might feel for Walter, his sister could never forgive her for the hurt she'd caused.

She smiled awkwardly, unsure how to convey her happiness. She had only ever wanted Imogen to be happy. Imogen had always wanted a little girl to bounce on her knee. She felt so very low. "Congratulations. I trust you are well."

"I am." Imogen's chin rose defiantly.

"I see." She took a deep breath as she inspected Imogen. There was no outward sign of her condition so she couldn't begin to guess when the babe would come. She would also most likely never see Imogen's child, and that made her terribly sad. It was really too late to make a difference, but this might be her only chance of mending any fences with the woman. "Would you excuse me a moment?"

She didn't wait for an answer, but rushed from the room and up the staircase. She raced to her bedchamber and grasped the handle of the first trunk stored under her bed. It was heavier than she remembered it being and she could only drag it from her room by one handle. At the top of the stairs she paused, listening to Julia plead with Imogen to stay a while longer. She eyed the stairs anxiously, but there was no help for the noise she would make and she had to hurry before Imogen left.

With a deafening clatter, she pulled the trunk down each tread. At the halfway point, she blew her hair from her eyes.

Valentine rushed up to her. "Melanie, what the devil are you doing with that trunk? You don't leave until tomorrow."

"I have to give this to Imogen. Would you help me carry it the rest of the way? She's in the parlor at this moment and about to leave."

Valentine grunted a little as he hefted the full trunk. He manhandled it the remaining distance to the parlor and departed, giving her a concerned glance. She had not time to explain to him what she was about to do.

Abigail caught her eye and suppressed a smile. She had already received her trunk a few months ago and had clearly guessed what this one also contained.

Imogen crossed her arms over her chest and scowled at it.

"Open it," Melanie urged when she did not move.

At Abigail's urging, Imogen slowly lifted the lid and let it fall open—to reveal a trunk full of children's clothes, and wraps, and blankets. Items all stitched by her own hand over the past dozen years; enough to last a child until they were toddling around on their own steam.

She had begun making small items for her friends at Andy's urging, and even though she had fallen out of grace since those days, she still made a few pieces for each year.

Abigail wiped a tear from her eye. "How is it you can do all of this? Mine was at least as large. You must have spent a fortune on threads and fabrics. Not to mention the hours involved."

She smiled. Since she'd never have children of her own, she had indulged quite a bit with her creations. "I enjoyed every stitch."

And if anyone had ever questioned her work, which happened rarely, it was always assumed she was making something for her own bottom drawer.

Imogen lifted the topmost piece and held it up to the light. This one had a twisting vine of lavender thread embroidered around the hem and small cuffs. It was one of her best efforts.

Julia poked through the contents of the trunk, her eyes widened. "You made all this for Imogen, and the same for Abigail?"

"Yours is upstairs," she whispered. "I didn't think it prudent to show you until you give my brother similar good news."

Julia beamed and hugged her arm. "You will have saved me."

"I will have saved the garments my nieces and nephews will wear from turning red from your pinpricked fingers," she laughed softly. She would be able to sew for Julia for years and years and send gifts by post.

She glanced at Imogen as she returned the garment to the trunk. Imogen had not said a word about her gift. Perhaps she expected too much.

Melanie closed the lid. At least she knew where she stood before she left Brighton.

"How could you do this to me?" Imogen's question had a rough edge to it.

"I apologize." Melanie dropped her gaze. Perhaps she should have asked Julia to deliver it after she was gone. "I thought to help so you would still have time to write."

Imogen's eyes widened and then she glanced at Abigail and Julia guiltily. Both ladies were frowning in confusion though and Melanie was puzzled. Did they not know Imogen and Brahms the author were one and the same?

The whole of Brighton was reading Imogen's work and quoting her at dinner parties. She'd always imagined them in on the great secret, but perhaps they were not.

Imogen grew pale. "What do you know of that?"

She shrugged. Imogen had been a talented writer even as a child. Back then she'd heard those stories firsthand, and later when they had grown distant, she'd discovered them in her brother's book collection and been pleased to know she'd continued. "I've always known."

"Imogen," Julia asked. "What is she talking about?"

Abigail appeared equally perplexed. Melanie swallowed, and glanced at her hands. She had blundered, and badly, yet again. Some claimed Brahms' work was too bold for young ladies to read. Imogen must be horrified by what she had almost revealed. And that emotion could quickly turn to anger toward her.

She struggled for an alternate explanation that might be the least bit feasible. This wasn't how she'd wished to spend her last day in Brighton. An idea struck her quickly though, one that was not easy to refute. "Lady Watson has been writing to my cousin in secret."

"To Teresa Long?" Julia asked. "Why is that a secret? I have written to her myself and told her how much we miss her."

Imogen nodded and then sighed. "I had hoped her heart had softened."

Julia appeared even more confused. "Softened from what?"

Melanie caught Julia's hand. "It was she who alerted my father to Valentine's behavior and ambitions. She wanted the easy life my father's money and position could bring. She couldn't bear the loss of stature, and did all she could to dissuade Valentine from going through with the marriage."

Imogen caught her other arm. "We didn't want you to be hurt by the discovery."

Julia collapsed onto the chaise. "Oh, I worked that out for myself ages ago. I thought at first she must have loved him, but it was only money she loved."

"She didn't want to lose." Melanie sank to her knees at Julia's side. "He never even realized what was truly going on. Not until the very last day before the banns were read."

Imogen nodded. "So all that time, Teresa claimed Melanie was against the match."

"She was lying," Melanie answered.

"She's surprisingly good at that," Julia scowled. "We all believed the worst of Melanie when the truth is quite different."

Melanie leaned forward and pressed a kiss to Julia's forehead. "I'll call for tea."

She turned to go and made it as far as the steps down to the kitchen before Imogen caught up with her. "Thank you for not revealing the truth."

"It is not my place."

"Who told you?"

"No one." She shook her head. "When I read your stories, I always hear you. I'll have tea sent up and ask Valentine to deliver the trunk unless you'd rather not have them."

"No, I want them." As she turned away, Imogen called out again. "Did you embroider any with yellow roses?"

"Of course not. You hate yellow and swore once you'd never allow the color on your children."

Imogen frowned at her then shook her head. "Thank you very much. They are beautiful."

Her spirits lifted a little. She might never be entirely forgiven, but she had made a start. It was enough. "You're very welcome."

"Melanie," Imogen said quickly. "Make sure you come back with the tea."

Chapter Fourteen

"I don't know what to think," Imogen exclaimed for the third time.

Walter had been home only a few minutes after making the rounds of his properties. He was weary and hungry and aching to see one person in particular.

That person was not his sister. But she was the topic of their conversation.

"It sounds to me as if you never lost Melanie's regard." He met his sister's gaze, and then sat. Imogen would want to speak of this for a while. The shock of receiving such a large gift from Melanie this morning clearly hadn't dimmed during the intervening hours. He had to hand it to her; Melanie was certainly full of surprises. She might not want children of her own, but she was excessively generous to have made so much for someone else who did.

Imogen sat forward. "Abigail tells me that she sent a similar-sized trunk to London two months ago, and there is supposed to be another tucked under her bed for Julia too."

He blinked. "Is there one for herself?"

"I don't know. She never ever discusses her own hopes with me in the room."

More than likely there was not anything for herself, and he was still disappointed in that. Her decision was probably made some time ago. "If memory serves, she has often sat in her parlor with a scrap of white linen in her lap. I never paid much attention to what she was doing."

"None of us did. I don't know what to do." Imogen stood and paced the room. "All this time I thought she'd forgotten me and she goes and does something *nice*."

Imogen bit out the word "nice" like it was an insurmountable inconvenience.

"You sound churlish about it." He sighed deeply. "Would you rather she changed back to the way she was before Valentine raced Julia?"

"No." Imogen sank into her chair again. "But she is different again since then too. Quieter, less opinionated. She defers to Julia, for heaven's sake!"

"Why should you complain about that?" He shook his head. "By your own telling, Mellie has spent hours and hours to provide you with clothing for your unborn child. What you have there is a sign of great love. For all of you."

"She knows I'm Brahms."

He grunted. He'd suspected but never had gotten round to confirming it. Few knew his sister was the author K.L. Brahms. It was supposed to be a well-guarded secret. He winced. "At dinner with the Mertons one night, one of your books was discussed, particularly *Findings from a Castaway* and the custard incident. She never let on then. What did she say about your writing?"

"Nothing untoward, and in fact she managed to change the subject so completely that Julia and Abigail remain in the dark even now. She must have assumed they knew about my secret writing life. We spoke later in private and she said she recognized my voice in the stories she read."

That could be quite awkward later. "I wonder if she knows you based the difficulties the heroine of *The Temple of Truth* faced on her experience with Percy McWilliam a few summers ago. It's a unique man who would propose twice in three years."

Imogen winced. "I hope not."

"Melanie is not stupid. If she read the stories then she could very well have pieced together the inspiration for more than a few residing in the township of Brighton, and made quite a fuss." That she hadn't, pleased him. "Perhaps you should not do that again."

Imogen collapsed back in her chair, her hands resting over her belly. "I am so ashamed."

He glanced to where her hands rested. "How are you feeling otherwise?"

"Happy."

"Good." He smirked. "I am glad to hear that Peter is keeping up his end of our bargain and being a good husband."

"He is wonderful." Her gaze narrowed on him. "All we need to do now is see you settled."

"I am settled." He stood and caught his sister's elbows as a knock sounded on his front door. "Don't even think of setting up another dinner and playing matchmaker again. I won't stand for it."

Imogen resisted his efforts to haul her upright. "Is that because you've someone in mind?"

"None of your business." He could tell her his hopes, but to do so would place undue scrutiny on himself and Melanie. He didn't think that a good idea yet. He was hoping to have a chance to talk Melanie around. They had something, or could have if only she were brave enough to trust his love and that everything would be all right.

"Might I suggest something to you?"

Imogen smiled. "Anything."

"Try again with Melanie. You might be surprised that what we thought of her past is quite wrong. Teresa Long embellished her flaws quite a bit, I've come to suspect."

He opened his front door to find David Hawke grinning at him. "Mr. George."

"Hawke. What a surprise to find you in Brighton. What is this, four times this year?"

"Five," he countered then tapped a folded paper across his palm.

Excitement gripped Walter at the sight. Could it be the information he'd requested from Hawke about changing his finances for marriage? Hawke had not written but Walter did not want his sister to know about his interest in marriage until the moment after Melanie agreed to be his. "Are you hand-delivering the investment information I asked for?"

Hawke's brow furrowed and Walter silently pleaded with him to play along with the pretense. At last the banker nodded. "Yes indeed. Everything you need to know."

The paper passed to his hand and he sighed in relief. He

nudged Imogen out the door. "Run along home now, little sister, and put your feet up. We have business to discuss."

Imogen gripped the doorway tighter. "But I didn't tell you the worst part. Does one nice thing and before I can get used to the idea I found out she's returning to Oxford. So inconsiderate."

"Whom are you babbling about?"

"Well, Melanie, of course. She leaves Brighton tomorrow. Valentine arranged it despite Julia being very upset to see her go. Melanie refuses to reconsider, even if she's obviously very sad too."

His stomach lurched. "That is news to me."

"I expect Valentine will tell you all about it tonight at cards."

He had other plans for tonight that did not need cards but was just as risky. He hoped to lure Melanie out tonight for another private conversation. "I must give my apologies, actually. I have something to do that cannot wait."

Imogen kissed his cheek. "Come and have luncheon with me tomorrow and tell me about your business. I'm hosting a small dinner tomorrow night, but there will likely be no chance for private conversation."

"No matchmaking, Imogen," he reminded her quickly.

She merely smiled.

As soon as Imogen slipped out, Hawke closed the door. "Why is Melanie Merton leaving Brighton if she's to be your wife?"

He did not know exactly, but he feared she was trying to run from her feelings. He sighed deeply and turned back to his desk. "She hasn't agreed."

"Not agreed? But I thought it was all settled. That's why I secured a license for you to marry."

He looked at Hawke in astonishment. "I didn't ask for that. You've gone to so much trouble."

"Our new partner at the bank has excellent connections." Hawke set his hand to Walter's shoulder and regarded him sadly. "Does the lady even know you wish to marry her?"

He shook his head and unfolded the paper Hawke had given him. He'd never seen a special license before. They were so rare outside of London. However, having one meant he could press his case without delay if he could catch Melanie first. "I wrote to you before I discovered she did not want children. Indeed, that is why she's refused so many suitors. She would refuse me for the same reason, I fear. You might have wasted a favor for this."

"So, no little heir to the George family fortune. Hmm," Hawke murmured before settling himself before the desk. "You couldn't change her mind?"

"I don't see how I can convince her in one night." He shook his head. "She is utterly determined on her path to live alone."

Hawke nodded. "Marriage is not an easy adjustment. Sacrifices must be made. Let me ask you this: what would you rather? Melanie, or to have children with someone else?"

Walter closed his eyes. The answer was so quickly presented in his mind that he almost swore. "Mellie, of course."

"That is what I thought you'd say." Hawke chuckled. "Let me know if I can be of any service for the wedding arrangements. I've not told my wife why we have come, by the way, so you still have the element of surprise."

"I might have to travel to Oxford tomorrow if I want to convince her."

"That's the spirit. Don't let her get away. As soon as I started reading your letter, I knew who your wife would be before I saw the name. An excellent choice."

"I hope you are right." When Hawke wandered out a few minutes later, Walter stared at the pile of correspondence on his desk. He didn't have much time to attend to his business before tomorrow if he intended to follow her but there were certain things he had to do.

He tucked the special license into his coat pocket and reached for the topmost letters. One was addressed from a Mr. Clemens of Southampton and it took a moment for the name to register. How could he have forgotten that the late Mr. Clemens had an older brother? He'd moved away many years ago and Walter had not heard him mentioned since.

He quickly scanned the note but then frowned at the message within. Mr. Daniel Clemens had written to enquire after his brother's widow and offered to help support some of the children. But his help came at a high price. Perhaps too high. He wanted to bring half of them into his home and had even chosen them by name. The two eldest were to be his.

Walter folded the letter slowly, astonished by such an offer. It would be hard for anyone to give their children away, but to lose so many, and at once. He scraped his hand over his jaw. He needed advice before he proceeded—and he knew just the woman to offer it.

He left his home and knocked soundly on the Mertons' front door. Valentine greeted him after a short wait. "Good afternoon."

"Hello there. I need to speak to your sister."

Valentine folded his arms across his chest. "Concerning?"

"Mrs. Clemens and her brood of children. I need her advice on a proposition I received in the post today."

Valentine frowned, clearly suspicious, but sent him into the parlor to wait while he went to fetch Melanie from above. He paced impatiently as the minutes ticked by, and only when she entered the parlor did he realize how much he'd feared she wouldn't see him.

His heart thudded hard against his ribs. "Miss Merton."

"Mr. George." She dipped a curtsy and bid him to sit. "My brother suggested you were in a hurry and needed advice."

"Not so much in a hurry but I do need your advice." He dug into his pocket. "I have a letter from the late Mr. Clemens' older brother."

"I did not know there was a brother."

"Estranged." He handed over the letter. "Mrs. Clemens does not read so the man, remembering our past connection, wrote to me instead when he learned of his brother's death. He has offered his assistance."

She unfolded the letter and frowned at it. "What sort of assistance does he offer? Funds? A larger home?"

"He's offered to take on half of the children and raise them as his own, if I've read that letter correctly." He bit his lip. "He particularly asked for the elder two."

Melanie held the letter to the light and read through the single page quickly. Her eyes widened impossibly by the end. "She'll never agree."

"I expected as much, and I do not particularly care for the offer myself." He shook his head. "However, I feel bound to offer her the choice and I am concerned she might feel pressure to comply in order to keep her current abode."

"You could be right." Melanie stared at him a long moment then looked down. "I saw her yesterday afternoon, and while she appears content enough in her new home, she also cannot stop praising you for what you've done to help her. She might feel obligated to lighten the burden on you."

She folded the letter and handed it back.

"I hoped you might be willing to visit her, break the news of Mr. Clemens' proposal, and lend assurance she did not need to take it. Her elder children are almost of an age where they will be able to find work soon. I'd like to help them stay together."

A brittle smile twisted her lips before she glanced over his shoulder. "Might I go with Walter, Valentine?"

He turned toward the door. Valentine lounged there, listening to every word of their conversation avidly. He nodded slowly. "Be back in one hour. Take the maid."

"Thank you." Melanie left to collect her bonnet and gloves while Walter fidgeted under Valentines curious gaze.

"No detours."

"Of course not." He wouldn't dare ruin Melanie's last night in Brighton by doing something she would regret. "I find I have to go to Oxford suddenly and I wonder if I might travel the distance with your sister tomorrow."

Valentine's shoulders sagged. "It would be a relief to have you travel with her. Her maid is going along as chaperone but it's a long way."

"Excellent." He dragged his gloves back on. "You have saved me the expense and bother of hiring a carriage for the trip."

Melanie rejoined them, wearing a warmer-looking coat today, and he was pleased she had listened to him.

Valentine nodded. "How long did you say you'd be staying in Oxford?"

Melanie appeared startled and he smiled tightly. "I'm not sure. My business depends entirely on someone else, but I am sure we can come to some arrangement sooner or later." He gestured to the door as the maid presented herself. "Shall we, ladies?"

The maid smiled warmly, but outside she fell back a few paces. "I hear Oxford is perfectly dreadful at this time of year," he mused.

"You cannot follow me to Oxford."

"You cannot stop me, and I have your brother's permission to see you safely home. He's agreed to let me travel in your carriage."

"To travel with me will call our connection into question."

"With a maid too, remember." He glanced over his shoulder. "I'm sure Miss Pond will beat me with your parasol if I overstep my bounds during the journey."

"I know my duty, sir," the girl promised.

He grinned, unsurprised by her loyalty to Melanie.

Once they were beyond sight of her home, the maid fell back a few steps more and he took a deep breath. "Imogen came to see me about you."

"She did?"

"Your gift for the child she carries truly startled her."

Melanie sighed. "I did not mean to make her uncomfortable but I wanted to know that she received the clothes I'd made for her children."

He lowered his voice. "We should discuss Brahms, too."

Melanie started to laugh softly. "And the mysterious Mr. Sandbottom? Could you not stop her from including you in her work with that description?"

"You discovered that too?" He glanced down at her in time to see a blush sweep her cheeks.

"Well, I would, since it was me who first described you that way to Imogen." She glanced down at her hands. "It was very wrong of me to call you names, but in my defense I was only a girl at the time. I never thought of it again until I read *The Recluse of the Sea*. She describes you very well indeed. It is my favorite story."

Melanie darted forward, headed toward Mrs. Clemens' home at a fast walk. So fast he had to jog a few steps to keep up. "There are many months left until the child comes. Why would you give it to her so soon?"

"I thought it might be the only chance I have to know whether she could forgive me before I go home."

"That might take time. Certainly more time than a single day, and I do think you have a chance to be friends again but only if you stay." He glanced ahead and saw Mrs. Clemens and several children coming to meet them. He had no time to make his case now so he finished with the truth. "Running away will solve nothing. Please. I'm not willing to let you go, Mellie."

Chapter Fifteen

———◆———

Ignoring Walter after his confession that he wasn't ready to let her go proved extremely difficult, but for Mrs. Clemens' sake, Melanie buried her heartache deep and focused on the task at hand. "It is not settled that you must give up your children but he has expressed an interest."

"No." The woman stood and turned her back to them. "My Francis never had a kind word to say about his elder brother. Said he was a bully as a boy."

"Sometimes what we perceive in childhood isn't always the truth. Perhaps he has changed." Melanie turned to Walter for his opinion. "What did you think of him?"

He described the man he'd known once. "His letter does sound sincere in his desire to offer aid."

"By stealing my children."

Walter stood. "I have your answer. Do not overset yourself. I shall write to him immediately and let him know you decline his offer."

Melanie caught Mrs. Clemens' arm and guided her back to a chair. "Kindly worded, of course."

"I will be eloquent."

He grinned and the pain of leaving him intensified. They worked well as a team. She turned her attention back to Mrs.

Clemens. "Now I want your promise that you will not fret over the matter. Walter has delivered his message and that is that. The children worry so when you become upset."

"I won't." Mrs. Clemens took Melanie's hand. "Promise me you will take care of yourself too. You will be a long way away and you'll be in my prayers every day."

"As you will be in mine," Melanie promised. She said her goodbyes and moved down the narrow hallway toward the front door to where her maid had waited. Walter followed close behind. He touched her shoulder briefly and an ache to seek comfort from him built. She always hated saying goodbye to her friends.

Words failed her and they returned to Cavendish Place in silence. Melanie was uncomfortably aware of Walter's presence so close and yet so far away, and while she'd love to stay in Brighton for friendship's sake, it would be impossible to change her plans now. Valentine would want to know why she'd changed her mind and she couldn't tell him. Her parents had already been warned to expect her arrival.

Her doorway loomed. "Would you care to come in?"

"I intended to."

In the entrance hall, he removed her coat and the brush of his fingers across her body sent a thrill through her. The maid smiled briefly then fled down the hall.

"Is that you, Melanie? Come quick!"

Her brother's wail sent her flying toward the sound. Valentine was bent over the settee where Julia rested, pale as a sheet. "What happened?"

"She fell from a window."

Melanie took a step back as nausea swamped her. Walter grasped her about the waist and hoisted her out of his way. He moved forward to inspect Julia. "Has a doctor been sent for?" he asked Valentine.

Melanie averted her eyes and held on to the nearest piece of furniture. She wasn't any good with the injured and sick. She never knew what to do and anything she said was tinged with panic. She peeked at Julia and her stomach dropped again. She was so pale and clearly in pain. Melanie shuddered and perspiration broke out over her skin.

"Her shoulder," Walter murmured.

"I tried to stop my fall," Julia whispered brokenly.

"Yes, darling." Valentine kissed her fingers. "I hope it is only dislocated."

A dislocation meant a resetting of bone into place. Julia would scream from the pain, and after that she'd be forced to rest for weeks and weeks. She would hate both things.

The door swung open and Brighton's apothecary, Mr. Rigby, hurried across to his patient. Walter returned to her side and put his arm around her back. She huddled against him, even as she fought her fear.

The apothecary peered at Julia over his spectacles. "I always wondered when I would have to come and call on you, young lady."

"Well, now you have your turn," Julia whispered. She moaned as the man moved her right arm. He wriggled fingers and toes and checked her eyes and tongue. By Julia's halting account, only her right upper body hurt.

"Dislocation of the shoulder," Mr. Rigby confirmed. He removed his spectacles carefully, his stare disapproving. "You are a very fortunate woman."

"I don't feel fortunate."

"It will be all right." Valentine smoothed Julia's hair from her damp face. His concern was sweet; a reminder that her brother wasn't afraid to show how much he cared.

"You'll be fine in no time," he promised. "I've seen this done before and every patient made a full recovery. Isn't that correct, Mr. George?"

"Indeed they have." The rumble of Walter's voice against her face had the immediate affect of calming her panic. She turned her face toward Julia.

"No limit of movement whatsoever afterward," Rigby crowed as he moved around her sister-in-law. "You'll have no trouble holding your babies when they come."

The mention of babies brought a smile at last to Julia's face. She took a deep breath and closed her eyes. Mr. Rigby and Valentine moved into positions to reset the bone. Melanie turned her face into Walter's chest as a sickening crunch filled her ears.

Walter squeezed her tightly. "She's fainted."

Unwilling to move, Melanie clung to Walter a little longer. He drew circles on her back and pressed a kiss to her hair. "The worst is over."

"Best get her up to bed and comfortable before she wakes from her faint," the apothecary suggested.

Walter set Melanie aside as Valentine lifted Julia into his arms. She did not stir and, with Walter's guidance, he removed his unconscious wife upstairs to their bedchamber.

Melanie drew in a steadying breath then faced Mr. Rigby. "Thank you, sir."

"It is my pleasure." He glanced at her curiously. "I thought you were made of sterner stuff."

Melanie shook her head quickly. "I never know what to do."

"Best remember to send for me when you have a need then. I was expecting you to faint." He collected his bag. "I'd best be on my way, but I will return tomorrow to check how she's doing."

As soon as Rigby went out, Linus Radley appeared on the front step, his eyes wild. "I came as soon as I heard. What has happened to my sister?"

"A fall." They had not spoken since she'd refused him, but she could not deny him the chance to comfort his sister at a time like this. "They say she will recover, Mr. Radley. Valentine is just settling her into bed upstairs."

She gestured for him to enter. He held his hat awkwardly and stared at her. Melanie took his hat just as Walter returned. "Radley," he said in a tone that was both cautious and belligerent.

"George. I've come to see my sister."

"Upstairs to the right. She was just coming round as I took my leave."

Radley took the stairs two at a time in his hurry.

Alone at last, Melanie locked the front door and pressed her head against the wood. She should have done something for Julia, but as always, her fear prevented her from acting.

"Mellie?"

She flew into Walter's arms and hugged him tight. "I should have helped."

"No. She is Valentine's wife. It is for him to fret and worry and comfort her when she is sick or afraid." Walter cupped her face. "Just as I comforted you."

He bent his head and kissed her brow.

Melanie curled her fingers into his lapels. He was more of a comfort to her now than he would ever realize. Even she had not understood until this moment how much she'd come to rely on him. He drew her into the parlor and pressed her into the chaise. When he took a place beside her and caught up her hand, she clung to him.

He shifted closer. "I expect this will curtail Julia's adventurous nature for a while."

"She's never been hurt before." Melanie bit her lip. "The odd scraped knee, but never like this."

"No. She has been very lucky. I hope this misadventure will put an end to her escapist tendencies."

"Perhaps it will."

He smoothed her hair behind her ear. "What did Linus say to you?"

"Nothing. He only came to enquire after his sister's health."

"He should have apologized," Walter grumbled and then stroked his thumb over her knuckles.

"Honestly, I don't need the apology and I don't want you demanding it." She took a deep breath and let it out slowly. "Could you stay a while longer?"

His smile was soft. "I wasn't going to leave until Radley was on his way home and I was certain you were feeling yourself again."

She smiled because he was the last man she'd ever expected to make her feel good about herself. Secure, safe. She did want his arms around her. His lips covering hers. His dry wit and teasing smile driving away the doubts that filled her mind constantly. She had grown accustomed to him, just as he'd suggested she might of a suitor.

However, he'd never said he was courting her. He'd never brought her flowers or taken her driving. Yet he knew her better than any of the men who had previously proposed. She wanted to show him how much she cared.

She glanced up at his face then leaned toward him, seeking a kiss. He obliged with a softly muttered groan and pulled her against him.

Walter brushed his lips across hers and she did the same back to him. She lifted her fingers to span his neck and pulled him even closer, settling her body against his, but he broke the kiss.

"I love when you touch me," he whispered against her ear. The warm tickle of his breath against her skin made her gasp. He brushed over her throat with the tips of his fingers and her senses rioted.

He eased away. "We should stop before your brother comes down and catches us. I've asked for tea to be readied for you and I think Valentine could use a drink to settle his nerves when he joins us."

He'd no sooner spoken of Valentine than the thump of boots on stairs reached her ears. She jumped to her feet guiltily as Valentine and Mr. Radley joined them. "How is she?"

Valentine ran a hand through his hair as Walter moved to the sideboard where the liquor was stored. "She's asking for you."

Melanie hurried from the room, regretful and grateful for Valentine's interruption. It was so easy to get swept away when she was alone with Walter.

She slipped inside the doorway of her brother's room quietly. Julia lay flat on her back staring up at the ceiling. A bottle of laudanum and a silver spoon sat upon a small table near the bed.

"Sister," Julia whispered.

"I'm here." A chair had been placed beside the bed and she perched on the edge. "What can I do?"

"Nothing for me. I have little time." She licked her lips. "You have feelings for Walter, don't you?"

"I…" Melanie nodded. "Yes."

Despite the pain, Julia managed a smile. "I thought so."

Melanie leaned closer and whispered, "How could you?"

"You have always preferred Walter's company and you were so sad after you quarreled."

"That was for many reasons."

A smile curved Julia's lips. "You were moping so much, I'm surprised Valentine didn't discern he was the cause."

"I was not moping," Melanie insisted, but whom was she fooling? She had lost her heart to Walter. His disapproval had cut her to the quick.

"You are a terrible liar." Julia winced. "I will be laid up a while, confined to bed they say, so I have demanded Valentine make you stay in Brighton for as long as I need you. That will be as long as it takes for Walter to propose."

She brushed her fingers over Julia's brow gently, surprised to see her hand was steady for a change. "You didn't fall out of that window on purpose, did you?"

"No. I'd never be as foolish as to purposely injure myself. I had not tried a window escape in this house from the upper floor and I'm sure I never shall try again." Julia licked her lips and closed her eyes briefly. "But I've been trying to dream up a way to make you stay and having no success. I like having a sister too much to lose you so soon. I'd rather lose you to Walter than to your parents. They don't love you like we do. Like he does. Miss Pond happens to agree with my assessment."

Melanie reached for Julia's left hand. "He has not proposed a marriage between us. He is not courting me."

"He will. He cares for you so much. I've suspected it for some time, and you care for him too, or you would never have allowed him to comfort you in his arms." Julia opened her eyes wide, but it was all too clear she was fighting the effect of the laudanum and losing. "I won't need you after nightfall. I will ask Valentine to stay with me so if you were to slip out of the house after dinner, he will never know about it. There is a lot more that can be said without a chaperone, a brother or sister, butting in at the wrong moment. That is how your brother convinced me to wed, you know. We spoke our hearts to each other."

"I don't think I should."

"Please." Her grip tightened. "He knows you. He knows what you want. Give him a chance."

Julia closed her eyes again and after a time, her breathing slowed enough to indicate sleep.

Was she brave enough to sneak into Walter's house just to talk to him? Nothing in her life had prepared her for making these sorts of decisions.

Assured that Julia rested comfortably for the time being, she slipped from the room and made her way to her brother, only to be brought up short. Linus Radley had remained with Valentine and Walter. She took a step back. "Julia sleeps now."

Valentine nodded and turned to Radley, one brow raised. "I believe you had something to say."

Radley cleared his throat. "I wish to apologize, Miss Merton, for my poor display of temper. I have no excuse."

Behind Mr. Radley, Walter nodded firmly.

She nodded too. "Thank you."

Although Radley appeared ready to say more on the subject, she lifted her hand to stop him. She did not want to hear his excuses for losing his temper. What he thought of her no longer mattered. "If you gentlemen would excuse me, Julia expects me to remain at her side until nightfall. Walter, could you inform Imogen of Julia's injury yourself? She should not suffer shocks in her delicate condition."

"An excellent idea." He collected his hat. "You know where I am if you need me."

Chapter Sixteen

———◆———

Repeated soft knocking brought Walter to his feet. He tossed Imogen's latest manuscript onto his bed and threw a shirt over his nakedness and tugged on a pair of trousers. At this late hour, close to midnight, there was only one reason for someone to seek him out. Trouble. He hoped the matter had nothing to do with Julia Merton.

He grabbed the candle from the bedside and rushed down the stairs to unlock the front door. As soon as he'd opened it a crack, he was pushed backward and a small shape darted inside his home.

"What took you so long?" Melanie gasped. "I was afraid I'd have to toss pebbles at your window to get your attention."

"I was in bed reading." He wasn't decent for company, least of all for Melanie's, so he buttoned his shirt quickly. "Melanie, what are you doing scarping around at this time of night without even your warmest coat on?"

"Seeking you out." She set aside her shawl and took the candle from him. "Should you not lock the door again?"

Walter closed and locked the door but he was confused. "Is Julia all right?"

"Yes, she is resting well." Melanie set the candle on the entrance table and drew closer, her gaze riveted to his. "Do you mind that I've come to see you?"

"Not at all." He caught her hand in his and squeezed. "But there are many reasons you shouldn't be here."

She glanced around the hallway. "Will you send me away?"

"No." He chuckled and brought her bare hand to his lips. "I want to see you all the time, but I'm running out of excuses to use with your brother."

She leaned into him, pressing against his chest. "I'm not leaving Brighton now. Julia needs me."

"I need you more." He pinched the wick of the candle, throwing the house into darkness. Through the thin shirt he wore, her touch was fire. He couldn't help his reaction to her. He brought his hands to her head and cupped her face. "What should we do about that?"

"I don't know. This is Julia's idea."

"Oh, I see."

"She suggested we needed to talk without interruptions but I don't know what there is to say now. I have never sneaked into a bachelor's home before. I've never done anything impulsive or scandalous in my life, and here I am doing everything I've ever disapproved of."

He sent silent thanks to Julia for her unexpected aid. "And you will never have to again, I promise."

He bent to kiss Mellie, still stunned that she'd risked her reputation to come and see him in the middle of the night, but so very pleased. In truth, he'd been wishing to return to her all evening to be sure she was still calm after Julia's injury.

Rather than continue at the front door, Walter caught her hand firmly, intending to lead her into his parlor. They could talk in the dark for an hour perhaps and he could steal another kiss or two before helping her return home unobserved.

"Should we not go upstairs to your bedchamber?" she whispered.

He snapped his mouth closed and drew closer. "Ah, Mellie. If we go upstairs, I won't stop kissing you. I'll make you mine and there will be no turning back for either of us."

She nodded. "I agree."

"You're sure?"

"No, but when I'm with you, I don't seem to worry about what is right or wrong. Everything makes sense when I'm with you."

"I'm so very glad to hear it." He scooped her up into his arms before she changed her mind. Melanie hugged his neck and rested her face against his shoulder with a sigh of pleasure. He carried her upstairs, directly to his bedchamber, and turned the lock once they were inside.

The room was dim, only lit by what little moon shone through the window, but perfectly warm from the fire. Since he'd been in bed when Melanie's knock had roused him, the covers were turned back. He released Melanie and set her on her feet.

There were papers scattered over his bed. Imogen's latest work should be packed away from sight. He gathered a few sheets together. "Another story of Imogen's."

Melanie smiled. "She has such a clever turn of phrase. The number of people who claim to know the author always astounds me."

"You kept her secrets. Thank you. Not many know about her work but if they did, I dread to think what would be said to her."

She grinned and handed him a stray sheet. "An easy task to hold my tongue. No one would ever expect me to know the author of such daring prose. She's almost considered notorious, which I'm sure she finds amusing."

Walter pulled Melanie against him. "What shall we talk about?"

"I have not stopped thinking about what you said to me about intimacy."

"Desire, kisses, touching." He grinned slowly, loving the feel of her against his body. He let his hand drift over her back and lower. "I must confess that when I saw you downstairs, I hoped you had come for me."

She nodded, and slid her hands up his chest. She teased the expanse of skin revealed by the loose fit of his shirt. "I don't know anything about desire."

"I will teach you the rest." He kissed her again, devouring kisses that made Melanie moan whenever their lips parted. He fumbled with the buttons on her gown and pushed the garment off her shoulders to reach her skin. Beneath, he found a light chemise but no corset. He drew back in surprise.

She blushed and glanced down. "I could not manage a corset without my maid's help. She would ask questions."

He lifted her chin and kissed her lips softly. "I'm not scandalized. I am delighted by your practicality."

"She has been looking at me so strangely since last night, and I discovered tonight she and Julia have been talking."

"They wonder about us?"

"They do."

"I was right. You are loved and belong here." He cupped her breast and tucked her hips against his. "With me."

She gasped, turning her face into his neck. Her lips brushed his throat and her hot breath drove him wild.

"Take down your hair for me," he whispered.

She smiled and moved to his dressing table stool. Her gown had fallen down her arms and she slipped them free so it pooled at her hips. Walter's breath caught at the arousing sight of Mellie half-dressed in his mirror. Through the thin chemise, her nipples were two dark patches teasing him.

As her hands rose to remove the pins from her hair, he dragged his shirt over his head and let it fall to the floor.

Melanie's soft gasp filled his ears and despite her inevitable blushes, he moved closer so she could see him. Her gazed fixed on his bare chest reflected in the mirror and her tongue darted over her lips to wet them. The way she stared made his cock thicken.

She shook her head then finished removing her pins, laying them neatly beside his ivory hair comb. She pushed her hands through the mass and let it tumble down her back in great dark waves. Her hair was almost long enough to sit upon and he groaned. He'd not expected her to leave it so long.

She stood but kept a distance between them as her gaze darted over his body. He kept his impatience in check, becoming anxious that she was disappointed. Once he had been tubby around the middle and he'd worked himself hard to lose the bulk and become fitter. He wanted her to like what he'd become. Slowly, she loosened her grip on the garment around her and it slipped down her legs.

He groaned softly as she stepped out of the prim gown and drew close to him. "Are you afraid?"

She reached to touch his chest tentatively. "Yes, but not of you," she murmured.

He brought her fingers to her mouth and blew over the tips, warming her. "Allow me."

He breathed over her fingers again, and then pressed her hand flat over his heart.

Melanie moved closer as she explored his upper body with a

gentle touch. "You are so strong."

"The swimming each day has helped."

Her brow creased as she stroked his chest, following the pattern of hair there. "Helped with what?"

Walter buried his fingers in her hair, and clenched the soft tresses at her nape. "Well, I was always rather round before."

"You were?" She shrugged. "I never noticed. You seem the same to me as you've ever been."

Walter was crushed that she hadn't noticed the improvement in his physique, but since her hands were sliding around to the back of his neck and over his shoulders, pulling him closer, he didn't complain. "My dearest, Mellie."

"My Walter." He curved his lips into a smile. "I like the sound of that."

She rose on her toes suddenly and brushed her lips across his. With urgency building inside him, Walter quickly divested Mellie of her chemise. Her breasts were pert, and perfect. Heaven against his bare chest. Walter hoisted her onto his bed and grinned down at her surprise. "I will remember this moment for the rest of my life."

He joined her on the bed and Melanie eased back, her head resting on his pillow, her dark hair fanned out around her. "I would expect no less of you."

She laughed then and Walter covered her, raining kisses over her cheeks, her nose and at last her lips. She curled her arms about his neck and held him tightly against her. Her body brushed against his cock and he broke the kiss to stare at her. With one hand and one foot, he nudged her legs apart. He could detect a slight increase in her tension and he smiled. "Trust me. I would never do anything to hurt you or make you unhappy. You don't want children and I will honor your wish. But you will be mine. Tonight and always."

"I'd like that," she whispered as her hands fluttered over his back as if she didn't now where to put them.

"But first, I want to kiss you everywhere."

He buried his face between her breasts and then moved to kiss one. She stiffened so he swept his hands over her chest and down her sides. He turned her over and then kissed every part of her back, including her bottom. When he rolled her over again, her face had taken on a fierce blush. She pulled him against her and they kissed and touched each other until they were both panting.

She touched his hip, resting her hand lightly over his trousers. "Only one of us is naked, Walter."

"I know. I wanted to take enough time that you would feel comfortable."

She laid her arm over her forehead. "I am entirely too comfortable like this. Please undress too."

He jumped to his feet and fought free of his trousers. His erection was curved against his abdomen.

When he met her gaze, her eyes had widened. "Now you see me."

She rose on one elbow, eyes fixed on his groin. "Oh my."

He climbed on the bed but kept a distance so she would not become concerned. "Speak your mind, Mellie."

"I…" She pointed. "That isn't going to fit inside me."

"You might be surprised to find that I will." He stretched to brush her long hair over her shoulder. "You will even enjoy me."

Her gaze flew to his. "I enjoy this. Being alone with you. Touching you."

She stretched to touch him next, her brow furrowing as her fingers slid over his erection. "So warm."

"I burn for you," he whispered. "And I'll make you burn for me too."

She moved closer to him, a bit nervously, and he wrapped his arms around her and simply kissed her for the longest time.

When her kisses grew heated enough that she was tugging on his hair, he pressed her onto her back and parted her legs. The apex of her thighs was concealed by a dark patch of curls and she tried to cover herself with her hands. "Don't hide from me, Mellie."

She slowly moved her hands aside.

He stroked over her there and then gently parted her folds.

Melanie jumped. "Walter?"

"Let me love you like this first," he whispered. "It will make things easier for us."

He lowered his mouth to her curls before she could protest. The touch of his tongue to her inner folds made her moan. He flicked his tongue over her slit and found her clitoris to tease. She moved restlessly until he gripped her hips tightly and he lost himself in her taste and her ragged moans. She muffled her scream when her release came upon her.

He rose up to meet her gaze, pleased and almost overcome himself from rubbing his cock against the sheets.

He took a moment to think of something unpleasant, eager to lessen his arousal before he claimed her.

However, she reached for him, hands beckoning him close.

When he slid against her, she buried her face in the crook of his neck. "That was not pleasant. That was almost too much for a body to bear."

He kissed her cheek and then chuckled softly against her skin. "That was only the beginning too."

Walter positioned himself and hovered outside her body. Anticipation was making him light-headed. He couldn't believe she'd come for him tonight and he needed her to come again. He slipped his hand between her legs and parted her folds carefully. She would be sensitive still, and she did jerk as he traced her cleft with the tip of his finger. Moisture had pooled there and he found her clitoris and stroked over it repeatedly.

When her hips rose to meet his hand, Walter placed his erection at her opening and set about to slowly claim her. An inch in and he was huffing. She was so tight, so much what he wanted. But he had to take this slow, make her enjoy their night together, make her understand that he deserved her trust and her heart the way she had his. But he had to keep his head at all times so he would withdraw before finding completion.

With all the patience he could muster, he worked his cock in and out of her body as carefully as he could.

"Walter?"

Conversation? Thank God for distractions. "Yes, darling?"

"Isn't it supposed to hurt more?"

He studied her face and saw absolute consternation reflected there. As he drew back his hips and eased into her again, he saw no sign of discomfort on her face.

Walter moved his weight to one arm and increased the pace of their lovemaking. He caught her breast with one hand and pinched the nipple gently. Touching her was heaven. She moved with him, a little awkwardly at first but soon enough her hands clutched at his sides, urging him on to love her with even greater passion.

Walter encouraged her to twine her legs about his, enjoying the slide of flesh against soft flesh. The added friction increased his desire. He studied her face, noticed her skin glistened, and she was panting along with every thrust too. Walter slid his hand between them and touched her clitoris again. The bud was large and Melanie's eyes widened as he stroked it firmly. He slowed his pace as her eyes shut and her fingers dug into his arms.

She stiffened suddenly, her sex fluttering around his cock with a second release.

A soft wail left her mouth, adding an additional threat to his good intentions.

He was almost too far gone in passion to hold back. He clenched his jaw as her tremors subsided and he was master of himself again, but he didn't imagine he could hold back for long.

When she relaxed, he set both hands to the bed on either side of her shoulders, lifted his body up and put his heart and soul into every thrust.

Her eyes opened and a tender smile greeted him. A shiver of desire stroked his spine as his release became imminent. He withdrew and turned aside just as his seed spilled from his body onto the bedding. When he was steady again, he gathered her close and groaned against her neck, completely overcome with intense satisfaction from their joining.

She struggled out from under him suddenly, her breath fast and rough. She put the whole of the bed between them—eyes wide with fear and trembling.

He waited till her breathing evened out then stretched to caress her cheek. "My Mellie forever. There's nothing to fear. I only wished to hold you a moment."

She slithered back toward him and collapsed on his pillows. "It was too much all of a sudden. I'm so sorry."

"I understand, Mellie. Truly I do." He eased close to her so they shared the same pillow. "Is it better if you hold me?"

"Yes," she sighed. "I would enjoy that."

He shifted and put his head on her shoulder. He caressed her breast and then let his hand rest on her belly rather than wrap around her. "You can hold me for as long as you like," he whispered. "And later if you want more, you only have to ask for what you need."

Her arms tightened about him, and she pressed a kiss to his hair. "I just need you like this, Walter. Just this and you."

Chapter Seventeen

As the sun set on Brighton at the end of another day, Melanie paced the parlor in her newest day gown, seething with frustration and troubling confusion. She had been uncommonly alert to every sound since daybreak had stirred the house, but the sound, the man, she'd expected to call on her had never arrived. She stared out the window in consternation.

Walter was late. Unbelievably late, in fact. She'd expected him to present himself at first light to speak to her brother and propose. She was dying to say yes to him. She loved him and he'd proved himself a man of his word last night.

She could marry him and not bear him children.

But she could not have a chance to say yes if he did not come to call in the first place.

Her sister-in-law eased into the room slowly, arm bound in a sling but dressed to go out. "I have the most extraordinary news."

"Shouldn't you be in bed?" Melanie snapped without thought then winced at how waspish she sounded. Melanie was always calm, always in control of her emotions, except when Walter George featured in her thoughts too heavily. She was annoyed at him for that. "Forgive me."

"If I am careful, I feel quite fine. No pain, thanks to the laudanum." Julia peered into her face and then smirked. "Did you not sleep last night?"

She had actually slept very well, with Walter in her arms or close by, and the rightness of their lovemaking soothing her senses. Except, she wasn't now sure last night was so perfect after all. When she considered the matter, it became obvious that at no time had Walter alluded to a desire to actually propose marriage to her. In anyone else she would say that she'd been utterly duped and she was beginning to feel foolish not to have sought that assurance before she'd climbed into his bed.

She bit her lip. She hadn't planned on ensuring her own ruin but that was precisely what she'd done.

"Well, my news is a treat for all of us. As you know, Valentine and I were to dine out tonight at Sir Peter's again but the venue has changed. Walter George has usurped his sister's plans to host a dinner and has invited everyone to him at the last moment. How extraordinary?"

So he was avoiding her now, too. She covered her face with both hands. Had last night been terrible for him? Had she not been affectionate enough to suit?

"I say, dear sister, are you well?"

Melanie jerked her head up. "I wasn't invited to dinner."

"Walter's invitation included your name, silly." Julia caught her hand and squeezed it. "He would never snub you."

Melanie's doubts remained. She hadn't seen him since the early hours of the morning when she'd slipped from his bed. Their last kiss had been sweet, but they'd not spoken about today. Could she pretend she wasn't in love with him enough to fool an entire room full of people?

"You look frightened," Julia whispered.

"That is because I am."

"Everything will be well. You'll see." She winked then turned to the doorway as Valentine appeared. "Always the last to be made presentable. Are you ready to go?"

Melanie glanced down at her gown. "I should change."

"Of course. We shall be fashionably late so you will dazzle him."

"Dazzle who?" Valentine asked.

"Never you mind," Julia quipped as Melanie slipped around them.

Although her hands were shaking, she managed to change into something more appropriate for dinner and restyled her hair with the assistance of her maid. She took one long last look in the mirror before squaring her shoulders and heading downstairs to join with her family. She followed her brother and sister-in-law from the house and along the short distance to Walter's front door in a state of panic.

Walter's occasional butler offered a ready smile as he took shawls and hats and bade them wait a moment in the hall to be announced. She glanced around anxiously. Could anyone tell that she had crossed this front hall last night and given her virtue to the man that lived here?

A shiver of that remembered desire stroked her spine now. She clutched her hands together tightly and wrestled her apprehension under control. What on earth could she say to him now? *Why haven't you proposed* seemed an inappropriate way to start any conversation between them.

The butler finally came to usher them forward. Melanie bumped into Valentine as he paused at the threshold, surveying an already filled room. Mr. and Mrs. Hartwood waved. The vicar did not. He stared at her so hard that she was certain he knew what she and Walter had done last night.

"Are we terribly late?" Valentine asked.

"You are right on time," Walter promised as he came forward to greet Valentine and Julia. They shook hands and he organized a comfortable chair for Julia. He stopped at her side, offered a wry grin that caused her heart to skip a beat. "Miss Merton."

"Mr. George."

He cleared his throat as he faced the room. "If I could have your attention. I suppose you are all wondering at your invitations. Please do thank my sister for being gracious enough to humor me tonight."

Imogen surveyed her brother with barely concealed curiosity. "Well, I don't know about being gracious. I am still waiting for an explanation and I reserve the right to be ungracious when I do finally hear it."

"I'll get straight to the point then." Walter cleared his throat. "I would like to announce a wedding."

Stunned silence filled the room and Melanie stared at Walter.

Linus Radley moved to the fore, eyes narrowing. "Whose?"

Walter caught her hand in his and threaded their fingers together. "Well, ours of course."

"But of course," Radley whispered with widened eyes. "I should have guessed when you thumped me."

Melanie couldn't keep her eyebrows from shooting upward in astonishment. "I never heard a proposal."

"Well, given your track record for saying no, I wasn't keen to go down on bended knee and risk being unlucky number thirteen," he shot back immediately.

Melanie blinked as she realized he was utterly serious. "You have to ask."

He faced her. "Not a chance. We are getting married."

Melanie couldn't speak.

"You are out of line, sir," Mr. Hartwood insisted. "The lady deserves a proper proposal or there can be no marriage."

"Walter, please. You cannot deny her this moment?" Julia cried out, and soon everyone else voiced his or her opinions on the subject too.

Embarrassment brought an uncomfortable heat to her face. This was not how she'd envisaged this moment. She had thought they'd be alone so she could tell him she'd changed her mind about marriage. He'd silenced her doubts about becoming his wife with his tender lovemaking and his actions to avoid pregnancy had been appreciated. But she couldn't discuss that here in front of everyone.

She glanced at her brother and saw confusion on his face. Valentine turned on his wife and regarded her suspiciously even though Julia ignored him and kept grinning. Melanie prayed he never guessed Julia had urged her to slip from the house last night.

As she was about to nod to cut off any further debate, Imogen's spluttering laughter filled the room. She risked a peek and saw Walter's sister double over in mirth—and soon everyone else joined in, holding their sides.

Everyone but Walter and herself.

Melanie wrenched her hand from Walter's, shame filling her. The situation was not at all funny. "I cannot marry you without first hearing a proposal," she whispered.

"Oh, stop, stop. This is no way to start a life together."

Imogen gestured to Valentine to join her and moved closer. "Let's see if we can speed this up for everyone's sake."

Valentine glared at Walter. "Walter, marry my sister."

"That is what I'm trying to do," Walter grumbled.

Imogen patted her brother's shoulder solicitously then faced Melanie. "Dearest Melanie, since my brother hasn't the wits to realize a sure thing when he sees it, I would like to ask for your hand in marriage on his behalf. He clearly adores you by making sure we were all here to witness this moment, and I for one want nothing more than to make you both very happy for all the days of your life. Please do us all the great favor of accepting him so we might all live peacefully ever after."

Despite the fact it was Imogen asking and not Walter, his eyes glowed with hope and an affection she had glimpsed in private these past weeks. She nodded. "Yes. I would like very much to be Walter's wife."

Their friends cheered and chatted among themselves, but Melanie only had eyes for Walter. She loved him and they would be husband and wife. She caught his hand and held it tightly. "I cannot believe you would think I might say no to you."

He caressed her cheek with a soft and gentle touch. "I have learned never to assume anything where you are concerned. You surprise me every moment, but I will give you the life you want because I want *you* more than anything else."

"Thank you." She leaned into his fingers, her mind making plans for what she needed to do in the next few weeks. "The banns can be called on Sunday and that gives us time to organize everything."

"Ah," Walter's face colored, "about that. I wrote to Hawke for advice and he delivered a special license on his arrival. We can be married today—tonight in fact, —if your brother is in agreement and we can come to terms. Mr. Pease is here to do the deed so there's no need to delay, is there?"

"Today?" Her mind raced. Her trunks were still packed in readiness for her aborted departure. Her parents were so wrapped up in their own affairs they probably would not protest about missing the wedding. She was of age to make her own decisions without deferring to them.

It was rather clever of Walter to have everything done so they could marry tonight. She frowned at that thought though. "When did you know you would propose to me?"

"I was never going to propose, but I decided I'd like you for my wife after our first kiss."

"And when did that happen?" Valentine cut in loudly.

Walter's smile was a trifle sheepish. "Close your ears."

They had argued not long after their first kiss. And yet, that still didn't explain his sudden decision to marry her. It made no sense. Unless…

She checked the location of their friends and family and, seeing none near, she leaned into Walter. "When did you fall in love with me?"

A shy smile crossed his lips as he smiled down at her as if she should know the answer already.

Melanie had known Walter almost her whole life. He was the only one she'd ever trusted implicitly not to overstep and as a child she had always liked to talk to him most out of everyone. He had always been there, in the background of her life, stepping in when a partner was needed for dancing or when she was uncertain. "A long time ago?"

"Yes, Mellie." His eyes sparkled. "A very long time ago. No doubt about the time you fell in love with me."

Her feelings for Walter had grown so gradually that she still wasn't sure when they had begun. Although she had loved her brother dearly, she had always envied Imogen and Walter's closeness. Had her feelings not been envy at all but the beginnings of a crush that she had misunderstood? She smoothed his cravat and stared up into his eyes as she accepted that her heart had been lost long ago, and she'd never realized that fact until this moment.

"Well, that is perfectly all right then. It is horrible to be in love alone."

Melanie rose up on her toes and kissed Walter full on the mouth before their family, their friends and the vicar. It didn't matter what anyone said about her behavior tonight. Walter had a special license and in less than an hour perhaps, she would be exactly where she wanted to be. Safe and loved in her Walter's arms.

Epilogue

A year and a bit later…

"Walter, you're being a stick-in-the-mud. Come and sit by me and take off your shoes."

He grinned at his wife where she sat alone on the seashore, removing her half boots and stockings in preparation for the night. The sun was just setting on another perfect Brighton day. It was a special occasion—the anniversary of their first summer, more or less.

Since their marriage, Melanie had blossomed and a decidedly bold and daring streak had taken over her nature. Many of the things she'd disapproved of before had been tried. Tonight's adventure was swimming—naked with him in the sea. He'd suggested it six months ago, but at the time it had been too cold. "I think everyone has gone home. We have the beach to ourselves."

She threw a heart-stopping smile his way. "Everything is perfect, my love."

His heart squeezed tight in his chest at the endearment and as she lifted her hands to the front of her gown, he smiled. It wasn't quite dark enough to remove their clothing yet so he plunked down beside her and put his arm around her back. "Ready for sunset?"

She set her head on his shoulder. "I am indeed."

Tonight, under the stars and a clear sky, the evening would look magical. Melanie naked—there were no words to describe how much he looked forward to those moments.

As the light disappeared, they stood and stripped off their clothing in the new dark. He caught his wife's hand and drew her toward the waves. He ducked under at the first wave, but Melanie wasn't so quick. She shrieked a little as it broke over her thighs, but eventually she ducked under the surface with a gasp.

Walter gathered her against him. Her slender thighs wrapped around his waist immediately and she held to him in the current. "That wasn't so bad."

A wave crashed over their heads and they both came up spluttering.

"Except for that," she twisted against him and the slip of her skin against his made him moan. Melanie chuckled wickedly. "Are you becoming aroused?"

"Everything about you does that, as you are well aware." He laughed and moved them into a patch of deeper water where the waves were not breaking. "I swear I'm a terrible influence on you sometimes."

Melanie grinned and kissed him deeply. "Well, I only became brave after you kissed me so you should be the one to reap the benefits."

He cupped her bottom and squeezed. "You'll have me out of my mind soon enough."

"Are you not going to swim?"

He cupped her breast next. "I couldn't possibly let you go long enough for that."

Melanie hummed softly and she reached for him. Her fingers closed over his erection and she stroked him lazily under the water until he was hard. Walter shifted his wife a little then pushed her down on his aching length.

After the cold of the sea, her heated core sent him a little mad with lust. There was no music but what they made together, and it was the sweetest melody he'd ever heard. He loved her for as long as he could, fondling her skin in the cool water, kissing her passionately. He couldn't get enough of her. He likely never would.

Melanie wrapped her arms tightly about his neck and brought her lips to his ear. Her hot breath over his skin brought on his release so quickly, he barely slipped from her body in time.

"I love you, Walter." Her grip tightened. "Why did you wait so long to make me your wife?"

He gasped for breath and teased her clitoris, satisfied only when she moaned deeply to his every stroke. He grinned as she shuddered violently in the grip of her release. Satisfied at last, he kissed her lightly. "The wait was worth it, my love."

"Indeed it was," she murmured and cuddled against him.

He held her tightly against him as he waded to shore with her legs wrapped around his waist. Adventure be damned. He would want her again and again, but back in their bed would be more comfortable for them both. He dropped her to her feet and wrapped her in a blanket so she would dry off. "I was prepared to wait my whole life to catch your notice and I'd almost lost hope until the moment you kissed me back."

"And I'd given up on love until we danced," Melanie whispered as she dropped the blanket and moved into his arms. "Partner with me again so I may show you how much I need you, Walter."

"Naked dancing?" He grinned and then laughed. "A woman intent on keeping my heart happy but there's no music to guide us yet again."

She grinned impishly and slowly brushed her hand from his hip toward his manhood. "We never did need music to dance well together."

He held her close and pressed a kiss to her hair. "Not even once."

The End

REBEL HEARTS SERIES

Book 1: The Wedding Affair
Book 2: An Affair of Honor
Book 3: The Christmas Affair
Book 4: An Affair so Right

SAINTS AND SINNERS SERIES

Book 1: The Duke and I
Book 2: A Gentleman's Vow
Book 3: An Earl of Her Own

And many more…

About Heather Boyd

Determined to escape the Aussie sun on a scorching camping holiday, Heather picked up a pen and notebook from a corner store and started writing her very first novel—Chills. Years later, she is the author of over thirty romances and has no plans to stop. Addicted to all things tech (never again will Heather write a novel longhand) and fascinated by English society of the early 1800's, Heather spends her days getting her characters in and out of trouble and into bed together (if they make it that far). She lives on the edge of beautiful Lake Macquarie, Australia with her trio of mischievous rogues (husband and two sons) along with one rescued cat whose only interest is that she provides him with food on demand.

You can find details of her writing at
www.Heather-Boyd.com